"I never even knew you noticed me,"

Thorn said.

"I noticed you," Alexandra admitted, laughing at the depth of the understatement. *I love you.* The thought came to her like words unspoken, filling her eyes with tears, blurring his features already heavily shadowed and indistinct. She lowered her head until their lips met again.

It felt right to kiss him, to have his hands roam her body. She wanted to be part of his life and his future and she wanted him to love her in the same, passionate, devoted way he'd thought he'd loved Natalie, in the same way she was discovering she loved him.

"This is wrong," she said at last, pulling away. Thorn was still obsessed with Natalie. And she couldn't make love with a man who didn't love her.

Much as part of her wished she could.

Dear Reader,

In 1993 beloved, bestselling author Diana Palmer launched the FABULOUS FATHERS series with *Emmett* (SR#910), which was her 50th Silhouette book. Readers fell in love with that Long, Tall Texan who discovered the meaning of love and fatherhood, and ever since, the FABULOUS FATHERS series has been a favorite. And now, to celebrate the publication of the *50th* FABULOUS FATHERS book, Silhouette Romance is very proud to present a brand-new novel by Diana Palmer, *Mystery Man*, and Fabulous Father Canton Rourke.

Silhouette Romance is just chock-full of special books this month! We've got *Miss Maxwell Becomes a Mom*, book one of Donna Clayton's new miniseries, THE SINGLE DADDY CLUB. And Alice Sharpe's *Missing: One Bride* is book one of our SURPRISE BRIDES trio, three irresistible books by three wonderful authors about very unusual wedding situations.

Rounding out the month is Jodi O'Donnell's newest title, *Real Marriage Material*, in which a sexy man of the land gets tamed. Robin Wells's *Husband and Wife...Again* tells the tale of a divorced couple reuniting in a delightful way. And finally, in *Daddy for Hire* by Joey Light, a hunk of a man becomes the most muscular nanny there ever was, all for love of his little girl.

Enjoy Diana Palmer's *Mystery Man* and all of our wonderful books this month. There's just no better way to start off springtime than with six books bursting with love!

Regards,

Melissa Senate
Senior Editor
Silhouette Books

Please address questions and book requests to:
Silhouette Reader Service
U.S.: 3010 Walden Ave., P.O. Box 1325, Buffalo, NY 14269
Canadian: P.O. Box 609, Fort Erie, Ont. L2A 5X3

MISSING: ONE BRIDE

Alice Sharpe

Silhouette
ROMANCE™
Published by Silhouette Books
America's Publisher of Contemporary Romance

This Book is Dedicated to My Most Loyal and Supportive Fan, My Mother, Mary R. LeVelle

A special thanks to Carolyn Deaton, Evelyn Lemon, Carolyn Moore and Pam Kreitzberg

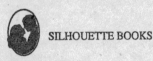 SILHOUETTE BOOKS

ISBN 0-373-19212-6

MISSING: ONE BRIDE

Books by Alice Sharpe

Silhouette Romance

Going to the Chapel #1137
Missing: One Bride #1212

ALICE SHARPE

met her husband-to-be on a cold, foggy beach in Northern California. One year later they were married. Their union has survived the rearing of two children, a handful of earthquakes registering over 6.5, numerous cats and a few special dogs, the latest of which is a yellow Lab named Annie Rose. Alice and her husband now live in a small rural town in Oregon, where she devotes the majority of her time to pursuing her second love, writing.

HOW TO GO FROM
BRIDESMAID TO BRIDE—
IN FIVE EASY STEPS

1. Be gracious. When your co-worker asks you to be maid of honor at her wedding, say that you would love to—even though you would *kill* to be in her shoes.

2. Be sympathetic. When the bride disappears, don't let the groom know that you are secretly overjoyed his "beloved" has flown the coop... and that you would eagerly take her place!

3. Be helpful. Volunteer to head the search party for the missing bride. Don't voice your suspicion that she has taken off with another man—one whose wallet is even bigger than his ego.

4. Be discreet. Keep smiling in the face of calamity. Resist the urge to explain why the maid of honor and the groom have checked in to the honeymoon suite—*together*.

5. Be persistent. And be optimistic! Your gorgeous groom is obviously the marrying kind. It's up to you to show him *which* bride is the right one for him!

Chapter One

It was a perfect day for an outdoor wedding. Early-June roses climbed the high rock walls of the enclosed garden; the sky was watercolor blue, the air sweet and warm. Eighty-eight people sat expectantly in white wooden chairs that were laced with nosegays of orange blossoms, forget-me-nots and pale yellow ribbons. A string quartet stood beneath a white-and-mint-striped awning, their gentle music floating out over the heads of the invited guests.

A perfect day for a wedding except for the fact that the bride was a no-show.

Alexandra Williams stood off to one side, partly hidden by a row of potted rose trees. As the sole member of the bride's wedding party, she was dressed in a pale yellow gown, a color so subtle, it almost didn't exist. She held a small frilly umbrella, which to her mind made her look like an extra on the set of *Gone With the Wind.* The handle of the worthless umbrella was encrusted with roses and ribbons. She'd done this herself; in fact, she'd created all the floral pieces that decorated the tables and chairs. She'd stayed late at the floral shop where she worked, up half the night as a favor for Natalie, the bride.

Speaking of Natalie...where in the world was she? Well, seeing as she was late for work half the time and tended to cancel appointments by simply not showing up, Alex supposed Natalie being late for her own wedding shouldn't come as too big a surprise.

Alex wasn't wearing a watch, so she wasn't sure exactly how late the ceremony was, just that the "moment" had come and gone. She glanced in the direction of the minister, who was standing by the groom's family. He was studying his watch, then darting quick looks toward the French doors leading from the house. He didn't cast the bride's family any loaded looks for the simple reason that the bride didn't have much family and what she did have wasn't there.

Alex's gaze darted ahead of the minister and rested on the groom, Thorn Powell. He seemed upset, a condition that didn't detract in any way from his startling good looks. In his tuxedo, with a vibrant yellow rosebud pinned to the lapel, his gray eyes stark against his tanned skin, his shoulders broad, his stomach flat, he appeared to be exactly what he was: a rancher in his early thirties, wealthy, smart, industrious—and about to marry the wrong woman.

No, no, no, Alex cautioned her runaway thoughts.

But they came again. Natalie and Thorn were wrong for each other. Alex knew it; she suspected Natalie knew it but didn't care, and now she wondered if maybe Thorn wasn't beginning to realize it, as well.

As if her thoughts had touched his mind, he turned just then, caught her eye and began walking toward her. Alex felt her heartbeat accelerate as his long stride brought him closer and closer. This was his land, his yard, and he crossed it with a self-assured gait and an intensity of suppressed irritation that wafted ahead of him like an invisible calling card.

"Alexandra," he said. "I don't suppose you have any idea where Natalie is?"

Alex shook her head, faintly aware of the tendrils of black hair that had escaped the French twist and now brushed her bare shoulders. "I haven't the foggiest," she said. "But you know Natalie."

"She didn't say anything to you?" he persisted.

"Not a word. Does this mean she hasn't called here, either?"

He nodded, then once again scanned the yard as though he suspected Natalie might be lurking behind a tree or a fountain. "When did you talk to her?" he asked.

"At the shop last night, right before closing." She didn't add what they had talked about: money. The fact that Thorn had it and Natalie wanted it. It had been mentioned so often, Alex had been moved to ask if there weren't other more compelling reasons to marry Thorn Powell—other attributes he might possess that made him the only man for Natalie Dupree.

"Sure," Natalie had said. "He's drop-dead gorgeous, too." A throaty laugh had been followed by the words, "And did I mention he's loaded?"

Thorn mindlessly punched fist against palm and said, "The limousine driver swears she was dressed in a wedding gown when she answered the door but that she told him to go on back to the agency, that she'd drive herself, that she had a phone call to make. I asked him if she seemed upset and he said she didn't, that on the contrary, she'd seemed to be quite excited—so excited, in fact, that she gave him a huge tip."

Thinking of the way Natalie refused to tip the kid who delivered sandwiches from the deli down the street from the florist shop, Alex said, "That's odd."

"Yes, it is."

"I imagine you called her apartment?"

"Of course." He glanced at his watch, surveyed the

yard, then turned that penetrating gaze on Alex. "I've called everyone I can think of. Now I'm going over to her place."

"What about all this?" Alex asked, a sweeping gesture including the guests, the towering cake, the musicians, the minister.

"To hell with all this," he said. "Anyway, it's about to be announced that the wedding is off, at least for today, and I don't particularly want to be around."

"Neither do I," Alex said heartily.

"Do you want to come with me? If she's there and she's healthy, she's going to need a bodyguard."

A smile crossed Alex's lips. She couldn't imagine this man actually hurting any woman, let alone Natalie, so technically, Alex was hardly needed. So why was her heart beating faster and why did her stomach feel all fluttery just at the mere thought of being alone with him? *You're crazy,* she told herself. To him, she said, "Okay."

She followed him out the back gate to a late-model luxury convertible replete with two long strings of cans tied to the rear bumper and a sign reading Just Married. The sides of the car were decorated with something white and gooey.

Although Thorn had been coming into the shop for the better part of two months to fetch Natalie for their various dates, the conversation Alex and he had just held was the longest they'd ever engaged in. It wasn't that he wasn't friendly and exceedingly polite; Natalie was simply always ready to leave. In fact, the store joke was how many seconds it would take Natalie to whisk Thorn out the door. So far, the record was thirty.

Thorn tore the sign and the cans from the bumper and dumped them in the back seat, where they landed with a rattle and a clank. Alex tossed her umbrella on top of the cans, then, with some difficulty, managed to stuff the bulk of her dress into the front seat and close the door.

As he started the engine, she slid a sideways glance at Thorn's profile, at the straight nose, the intent mouth, the assertive thrust of his chin. Every line and crease shouted impatience. She looked away as he backed the car down the long drive and pulled onto the road. As distracted as he was, he was also a good driver, and the trip from his place to Natalie's apartment building took only fifteen minutes.

The complex was in a nice area of the small city of Cottage Grove, nestled next to a park, which currently held several children involved in a game of softball. As Alex unfolded herself from the front seat and spilled onto the pavement like a wilted rose, she sensed the children staring. With Thorn in a tux and her in a gown, they must look like the misplaced top off a wedding cake. This thought was followed by an inward smile she didn't stop to dissect.

"Her car isn't here," Thorn said.

Alex looked across the sea of automobiles. "How do you know?"

"They have assigned parking spots. I just parked in her space. Come on. Her apartment is on the second floor."

Thorn stood aside for Alex to mount the stairs ahead of him; she lifted her skirt in her hands and began making her way, with him close behind her.

The landing was made of the same concrete as the stairs, a no-nonsense iron railing added to keep tenants from taking a nosedive to the parking lot. Alex's heels clicked along the walk as she passed the windows of different apartments, some decorated with potted plants, one with a cat sitting on the sill, catching the afternoon sun.

"Hey, you passed her door," Thorn said, gripping Alex's elbow and halting her progress. "It's this one—3B. Haven't you ever been here before?"

"No," she said.

He regarded her with a startled look, which he shook off with effort as he reached past her and rapped on the metal door. They waited expectantly for several seconds, then he knocked again, this time so hard, the curtains in the next apartment parted and an elderly woman peeked out. Alex smiled reassuringly at the woman who snapped the curtain shut without changing her expression.

"Friendly place," Alex murmured as she watched Thorn take his keys from his pocket. He found the one he was looking for and inserted it into the lock. The door opened easily, soundlessly.

"Nat?" he called into the dark room.

No answer. He propelled Alex inside and closed the door behind him; they were instantly swallowed by darkness. She stepped backward and ran into him. He clutched both her arms and steadied her, then dropped his hands and patted the wall, looking for the light switch. The room was suddenly flooded with light.

Alex ran her hand up and down her arm where Thorn had touched her. He had his back to her and was leaning down to press a button on the answering machine. As his recorded voice filled the room, pleading with Natalie to pick up the receiver, Alex looked about, registering a beige sofa, tan carpet, creamy drapes, ivory pillows. The place was exceptionally neat.

Thorn had left three messages, each one reflecting increasing alarm. He flicked off the machine after the final message and faced Alex.

"I don't know what to do," he said.

"Maybe we should call the hospital—"

"I already did that. I also called the emergency clinic and the police, who told me to call back in twenty-four hours if I still haven't heard from her."

"Then maybe we should go back to your place and wait. I know this may sound silly, but I have a feeling there's a perfectly logical explanation—"

He waved aside her assurances. "You're her best friend. What about her family?"

Alex was immediately uncomfortable with the tag of "best friend," although technically, she supposed it fit. Natalie had lived in Cottage Grove for less than a year and had worked in the shop just six months; as far as Alex could tell, she had few female friends. "You're her fiancé," she shot back. "If you don't know about her family, how in the world would I?"

"Don't you women talk to one another about things like that?"

"Don't people about to commit their lives to one another exchange a little family information?" she countered.

He cast her an irritated glance and sighed. "I know her mother is dead and she's estranged from her father. I know that she invited less than a dozen people to the wedding and half of them were from the flower shop. That's all I know."

"Well, Thorn, believe it or not, that's all I know, too. Let's go—"

"Not yet. First we'll take a look around here for a note or some kind of indication as to where she might be. You take the bedroom, I'll take the living room and the kitchen."

Alex found the bedroom at the end of a short hallway. Like the living room, this room was tastefully decorated in a bewildering array of beiges, but unlike the bulk of the apartment, it was amply lit with a large window and a skylight making artificial illumination unnecessary.

She caught sight of herself in the mirror above the dresser and winced. The dress had not been her choice. The color did not flatter her dark eyes and hair and tended to wash out her skin tone. She had argued that it looked too bridelike, sure that Natalie would immediately switch her to bright blue or pink, but Natalie had just smiled and said, "It looks expensive. I like it!"

"It is expensive," Alex had said, gulping when she got a look at the price tag. There was no swaying Natalie, however, and in the end, Alex had put a down payment on the yards and yards of flounce and fluff, knowing she'd never wear it after Natalie's wedding.

Ah, she thought now. *What I wouldn't give for a pair of jeans and a tank top.*

She felt like a trespasser as she opened a few drawers, coming away with the distinct impression that many items were missing. A peek in the closet confirmed that suspicion. There was a long rectangular impression left in the plush carpet that had to have been left by a suitcase. The clothes rod was half-bare.

So what? Natalie had packed for a three-week honeymoon in Hawaii. She'd talked of little else for the past month. She'd painted a picture of tropical nights and fragrant orchids, a picture only slightly marred by her continual reference to the first-class air tickets Thorn had booked and the deluxe suite they would enjoy once they got there.

A final glance around the room revealed a telephone by the bed and another answering machine. The telephone had a different number printed on the receiver, meaning Natalie had two separate phone lines. The message light was not blinking, but for some reason, Alex pushed it anyway. A mechanical voice informed her it would replay messages.

A male again, but not Thorn. This voice was lower pitched, older. *"Nat, honey, you win. Meet me at Otter Point, we'll go from there."*

Otter Point was on the Oregon coast. Alex had been there many times, though she'd never stayed in the luxurious hotel overlooking the cove, not with the prices they charged, not on her salary. But the beach was free and she loved to climb the black rocks and listen to the pounding surf. She rewound and replayed the message, glad that Thorn hadn't heard it, undecided as to how to relay this piece of information.

"Play that again," Thorn said from the doorway.

Alex swiveled around. His face was expressionless, but

his eyes were like lasers as he stared at her, one hand on the doorjamb, the other in his trouser pocket. "Play it again," he demanded.

She played it again.

"Damn her," Thorn said.

"Now, Thorn, don't jump to conclusions," Alex cautioned.

"Jump to conclusions!" he yelled. He regained his composure and added, "I'm afraid I don't see too many ways to interpret that message. Besides, you haven't seen what's in the hall closet."

"Maybe that was her dad on the phone," Alex said.

Thorn looked doubtful, but he said, "Play it again. Please."

She played it yet again. The words were nebulous enough to leave the possibilities wide open, at least in Alex's mind.

"I don't think it's her father," Thorn said. "He sounds old enough, but there's some other quality to his voice I can't pin down, except that it's not paternal." He took a step into the room and added, "The message sounds very personal to me. Damn! I think Natalie has flown the coop to hook up with whoever that is on the phone."

This was the first thought that had crossed Alex's mind but now she wasn't so sure.

"If it was her father, why wouldn't she have called the house or left me a note?" he added.

Alex shrugged. She wanted to say that Natalie was self-centered and that if something caught her attention, it was entirely possible she would forget all about Thorn, but she kept hearing Natalie talk about Thorn's money. It was hard to believe she'd walk away from that and yet, apparently, she had.

Alex imagined that being stood up at the altar—even if it was for a long-lost father—would be hard for anyone to take, let alone someone like Thorn Powell, who had probably never been stood up in his entire life.

"Come look at what I found," he said.

She followed him into the hall, where a narrow door stood open revealing a small closet. Heaped on the floor of the closet was Natalie's wedding gown, tossed aside like a used tissue.

"Oh, dear—" Alex began.

"Still think she ran off to meet her father?"

"Well—"

"Because I'm having a hard time swallowing that scenario. She's dumped this dress the same way she's dumped our wedding, the same way she's dumped me."

"I admit it looks that way, but—"

"She's not going to get away with it," Thorn said suddenly and, turning on his heels, walked down the hall, Alex once again in hot pursuit.

"What are you going to do?" she called.

Ignoring her, he tore open the front door and disappeared outside.

Alex closed and locked the door behind her, then raced along the balcony to catch up with him. At the top of the stairs she hooked the toe of her right shoe in the hem of her long skirt and, for one terrifying second, thought she was going to end up at the bottom of the steep concrete stairs in a broken heap of torn silk and shattered bones. Gasping, she threw out her hands for balance and toppled forward.

Thorn wheeled and caught her with steady hands. Effortlessly, he swooped her into his arms and carried her down the stairs.

"This isn't necessary," she mumbled to his chin.

"I don't have the time to cart you to the hospital," he said. They had reached the ground and for one long second, he stared down into her eyes. The gray of his irises seemed fogged with doubt. Alex guessed this was an uncomfortable condition for him, that he wasn't used to indecision.

He unceremoniously put her down on her feet.

"Thorn, what are you going to do?"

The confusion in his eyes fled like a flock of birds suddenly startled. "I'm going to find her," he said. "She's going to tell me what's going on or I'm going to wring her pretty little neck."

"But—"

"No buts."

"Then I'm going with you," Alex said firmly. Natalie wasn't her best friend, and Alex certainly didn't admire the way she was treating Thorn, but there was a murderous look in his eyes.

"No, thanks," he said as he strode toward his car. She reached the passenger door as he slid in behind the wheel.

"You can either take me with you or I'll follow you," she told him.

"How? You don't have a car."

"You're right. If you leave me here I'll be stranded."

"Call a cab," he said as he put the key in the ignition.

She held up both empty hands. "How? I don't have a penny on me."

He shoved a hand in his pocket, then swore. "Neither do I," he said.

"Listen, my feet are killing me and this bickering is just wasting time."

He stared at her again, as though seeing her for the first time, then shook his head and heaved a sigh. "You're right, it is. Okay. Just get in."

Alex once again folded herself into the little car. She didn't stop to wonder why she was foisting herself upon this poor man; she only knew that she felt compelled to accompany him.

After all, I'm the maid of honor, she mused, though she was pretty sure no etiquette book counted among the official duties hunting the bride down like one would a rabid dog.

"Fasten your seat belt," Thorn told her as he drove the car through the winding streets.

She did as he asked—no mean feat, given that the dress increased her girth threefold—and said, "Where are we going?"

He shot her a quick glance with eyes that now brimmed with life. Alex realized he was a man used to taking action, used to dealing with a crisis by controlling it.

"Otter Point. Where else?" he said briskly.

Where else indeed?

Chapter Two

Thorn made himself obey the speed limits, though every fiber of his body urged him to press the accelerator pedal right through the floor. When he'd checked his pockets for a quarter to give Alex to call a taxi, he'd realized he'd left the house not only without any loose change, but without his wallet. With no driver's license in his possession, all he needed now was a cop with a quota to fill.

He stole another sidelong look at the woman seated beside him. She was staring straight ahead, her hair still partly piled on top of her head, her profile as distinct as a cameo. He had noticed her in the flower shop, had even wondered about her a little as she seemed so wrapped up in her work, her fingers deft, her concentration complete. But truth of the matter was, he'd been so centered on Natalie that this young woman had been little more than an attractive fixture in among the blossoms. She was as pretty as her flowers, he now noted, her skin as translucent as a petal, her lips full, her lashes black and long, her eyes a startling shade of dusky blue.

She seemed to sense him staring at her and turned her

head slightly, shooting him a quick nervous smile as she attempted to brush windblown strands of glossy dark hair away from her eyes. He guessed she was suffering second thoughts about the wisdom of accompanying him on this fool's errand.

"There's a scarf in the glove compartment," he said.

Alexandra nodded slightly and retrieved the scarf. It was Natalie's, of course—white and filmy, the stuff wedding gowns were made of. Thorn felt a small knot form in his throat as Natalie's perfume hit his nostrils and then was gone. In his mind's eye, he saw the crumpled dress in Natalie's closet, the one she'd refused to let him see before the ceremony—hell, the one she'd bought with his money!

Maple and alder branches intertwined, forming canopies above the winding road that led from Cottage Grove to the Oregon coast. The river ran beside the road in places, and Thorn caught glimpses of people leading ordinary lives on this clear Saturday afternoon—swimming in the river, fishing, boating, picnicking.

"How could she do this to me?" he asked, not realizing until he heard Alexandra answer that he'd said it aloud.

"You're assuming she's done something wrong," she said.

"Yes, I am. Humor me."

"I don't know the answer," she mumbled.

"I've given that woman everything she wanted."

"Well—"

"And she has wanted a lot, trust me," he added. He shook his head and glanced briefly at Alexandra. "You didn't know about this other guy?"

"No," she answered. "If there is another guy."

"There's another guy."

"Assuming there is," she said cautiously, "didn't you suspect something was wrong?"

He shook his head again and then found himself pondering the question. The truth of the matter was that he and

Natalie had never really talked much—it hadn't seemed necessary. Words were for other people, for family and friends and business associates, not lovers. At least, that's what he'd always thought, and Natalie had seemed to be in perfect harmony with this ideology.

"I know you were anxious to get married," his passenger continued, "but maybe you should have given her more time. Maybe this whole thing is a blessing in disguise. Now you'll have a chance to really talk to each other about how you feel— Yikes, Thorn, you're awfully close to that bumper up ahead!"

He eased off the accelerator. "What do you mean, you know I was anxious to get married?"

"Natalie told me."

"Natalie told you what!"

"That she wanted to wait a few months, but you insisted on a June wedding. She thought it was very romantic. Actually, everyone in the shop thought it was romantic."

He furrowed his brow and shook his head, but he didn't say anything. A subconscious thought surfaced like a dead guppy in a fishbowl. *Did he really know Natalie Dupree at all?*

The closer they got to the ocean, the chillier it became. Determined not to add to Thorn's concerns, Alex shivered in her flimsy dress and didn't ask him to put up the top of the car. The scarf helped keep her head moderately warm, and she found that she could half bury her bare arms in the voluptuous folds of her skirt.

At least her feet didn't hurt anymore. She'd flicked off her shoes as soon as she got in the car and now she wiggled sore toes against the plush carpet, suspecting there was no way on earth she was ever going to get those pointed instruments of torture back on her feet.

It was early evening by the time they broke onto the coastal road and turned north. Alex knew it would take at least another hour of steady driving to reach their destination, and she clenched her teeth together to keep them from chattering. Thorn was driving at a much more moderate speed than she would have predicted. In a way, she wished he would speed up and get this drive over with.

For the first time, she began to wonder what exactly would happen when they reached Otter Point. Should she trail behind Thorn as he looked for his wayward bride, or should they separate and cover twice as much ground? No, she'd better stay close to him, at least close enough to act as a buffer so that Natalie didn't have to face Thorn alone.

Actually, what she really wanted to do was to plant herself in the hotel lobby, preferably near a functioning heater vent. Maybe she should broach this subject now and together they could settle on a plan of action.

One short peek at Thorn quelled that notion. His features were set in a frown that suggested whatever events he was mentally reviewing weren't happy ones. She decided she had no desire to interrupt his thoughts and looked ahead instead, anxious only to get this over with.

After a long, slow curve, the road straightened out and ran beside the beach. Only a few determined walkers and people throwing sticks for frantic dogs were visible. The promontory on the north end of the beach was called Otter Point, and even from a distance of two miles, Alex could make out the hotel, which appeared to cling to the rocks with the tenacious grip of a limpet. The tiers of decks jutting from the main structure were outlined in twinkling white lights, while the interior of the hotel glowed yellow in the gathering dusk.

"We're almost there," she said.

Thorn spared her half a glance but said nothing.

"Do you have any idea what you're going to say to her?" Alex persisted.

"No."

She took the hint—the man did not want to talk, at least not to her.

Thorn stopped the car opposite a pair of wide glass doors etched with seabirds. Within seconds, a young man in a teal green uniform appeared, opening Alex's door, offering her a hand. Stiff from the long ride and chilled through to the bone, Alex knew her exit from the car was something less than graceful. As she unwound the scarf from her head, she felt half her hair tumble to her shoulders and looked up to find her helper, whose name tag identified him simply as Roger, staring at her with a bemused smile.

She reached back inside and grabbed her shoes. By the time she'd straightened, Thorn had come around the car and was waiting on the curb for her.

"Any luggage, sir?" Roger asked.

"What?" Thorn grumbled as he fished in his pocket.

"Luggage, sir?" Roger repeated.

Thorn, looking distracted, said, "No. I mean, yes. In the trunk."

Alex looked at Thorn. "You brought luggage?"

"Honeymoon," he snapped.

"Oh."

"And I guess I'll have to catch you later," Thorn added as he turned back to Roger, his hands empty.

"That's fine, sir."

Another uniformed teenager had slid in behind the wheel to whisk the car away to parts unknown. He added, "We understand, sir," and followed the comment with a broad wink.

"Understand what?" Thorn asked impatiently.

With a pointed look at Alex, the one in the car said, "How it is, you know, on your wedding day and everything."

Alex opened her mouth to speak but a swift shake of Thorn's head silenced her.

Roger gestured at the convertible. "You know, sir, this

goop on your car can't be good for the paint." Nodding at the driver, he added, "Me and Todd would be happy to wash it off for you."

"Yeah, no problem," the driver said.

Thorn looked at the two younger men as though they were speaking Greek, and Alex realized these mundane concerns were beyond him at the moment. Taking matters into her own hands, she said, "Great."

Thorn grabbed her arm and steered her through the doors, into a huge lobby decorated in a dozen shades of blue and green, the colors of the sea. Without saying a word, he strode purposefully toward the reception desk, Alex struggling to keep up with him. She hadn't yet had a chance to put on her shoes and without the heels to add another two inches to her height, the dress dragged awkwardly on the floor.

The desk clerk was a woman in her twenties with enough blond hair for two people. She swept tousled bangs away from her eyes as she watched Thorn approach, then moistened her lips with a quick flick of her tongue. Her name tag read Candy.

"What can I do for you, sir?" The question was uttered in a voice that suggested the possibilities were endless.

"I want to know if you have a Miss Dupree registered," he said. "Natalie Dupree."

As Candy punched a few keys on the computer, Alex snuck a peek up at Thorn's face. His gaze was directed solely on the clerk, or to be more specific, solely on the clerk's hands. She wondered if Candy was aware of the tension building in Thorn's body as he watched her red nails click against the plastic keys, seconds passing so slowly, each seemed to have a separate identity.

At last, Candy chirped, "No, sir. I'm sorry, but no one by that name is registered here."

Alex, amazed, said, "Are you sure?"

"Quite sure," Candy said without so much as a glance at Alex.

"Wait a minute," Thorn said. "Maybe she's using a different name. She's about this tall," he explained, holding his hand below his chin, "with reddish blond hair and green eyes. She's twenty-six years old."

"I'm sorry, sir—"

"She may be with someone else," Thorn said reluctantly.

"I'm sorry," Candy repeated as Roger appeared at Thorn's elbow, a brown leather suitcase clutched in his hand. "I just came on duty a few minutes ago. I haven't seen anyone fitting that description."

"Fitting what description?" Roger asked.

Once again, Thorn described Natalie, this time adding the make and color of her car, but he was met with the same blank stare. "'Course, I've only been here since six," the boy said, "and there's a billion cars down on the extra lot."

Thorn swore under his breath.

Candy, staring at the suitcase, said, "Are you staying with us? Do you have a reservation?"

Thorn once again looked baffled by a couple of simple questions. Apparently, he'd been so positive Natalie was registered at the Otter Point Inn that he was temporarily set adrift when he found out she wasn't. As Alex had no idea what he wanted to do next, she decided to keep her mouth shut.

Roger, however, was not bound by these same concerns. "They're on their honeymoon," he told Candy, "in one gorgeous car."

Immediately breaking eye contact with Thorn and sliding Alex a brief glance, Candy said, "How nice."

Alex blurted out, "Not really—" but stopped as she noted the two startled expressions that greeted the beginning of this sentence. To heck with them, she thought, vowing once again to stay quiet.

"Well, by chance, the honeymoon suite is open," Candy said as she scanned the computer screen. "As a matter of fact, it's our only vacancy. We had a late cancellation."

Thorn looked down at Alex. For a second, the rest of the world seemed to recede as his eyes probed hers. At last, he said, "Do you want me to drive you back to Cottage Grove or shall we take the room for a night and think this thing through?"

While two gaping strangers looked on, Alex stared at the man standing in front of her and wondered if pride alone was keeping him on his feet. His eyes looked drawn and tired, his square shoulders sagging under the continual blows to his ego. She smiled and said, "Whatever you want, Thorn. You call it."

He looked back at Candy. "I don't have my wallet on me. We left in kind of a rush." Candy looked at him as though waiting for more information so he added, "Hell, just call Peter Hanks. He'll vouch for me."

"You want me to call our manager?"

"Please. Tell him Thorn Powell is here. He knows who I am."

It took a little convincing, but in the end, Candy did call the manager at his home, where he apparently vouched for Thorn.

"I'm sorry to put you through all this, Mr. Powell," the clerk said after she hung up the receiver. Her manner had moved from flirtatious to respectful, a subtle shift, but noticeable to Alex.

Thorn shrugged as though it was of little concern to him. Alex couldn't help but notice how the dynamics of the situation changed once Thorn's last name was known, and she wondered how often he stayed here and with whom—

"We'll run a tab for you, sir," Candy said as she handed

Thorn a room key and a piece of gold plastic that looked like a credit card. "This is good in any of our restaurants or shops. Please, enjoy your stay." With an ingratiating smile she added, "And I'm sorry I didn't recognize you, sir. I've been here only two weeks—"

"Since I haven't stayed at the inn for over six months, I don't suppose you should be required to know me on sight," Thorn grumbled.

Candy's answering smile was as sweet as her name and was gone just as quickly as she turned her attention to Alex. "Congratulations on your marriage," she said.

Alex knew what the clerk was seeing: a disheveled woman in a gaudy, droopy gown, barefoot, with hair going in twelve different directions. She knew that without prior knowledge of the situation, the conversation she and Thorn had held discussing whether they should stay or leave must have sounded very odd coming from a supposedly newly-wed couple. But she didn't like Candy's challenging stare or the condescending tone of the woman's voice, so, crinkling her eyes, Alex looped her arm through Thorn's arm, and said, "Thank you ever so much."

Thorn's brow wrinkled as he glanced down at Alex.

"Let's go, sweetheart," she added.

Shaking his head, Thorn led her to the elevator, one step behind Roger.

The car was the topic of conversation as they rose to the third floor. Roger carried the ball while Thorn grunted now and then and Alex stopped to consider what she'd just agreed to—namely, spending the night in the same room with Thorn. She'd dropped his arm the minute the elevator doors closed, and now she snuck him a clandestine look and bit her lip. She wondered why she was allowing herself to be swept up in this man's life and what he would expect as far as sleeping arrangements were concerned. After all, he was a stranger.

They followed Roger down a hallway, waiting patiently

while the young man opened the oversized door of the honeymoon suite. As he switched on various lights and set the suitcase on the small cherry trunk at the foot of the bed, Alex stood off to the side, looking around the huge room, her shoes clutched against her chest.

Four glass doors opened onto a balcony, which apparently faced the sea. The wallpaper was a collage of cabbage roses; the bed was covered with deep pink satin and a dozen lace pillows, and there were silk flowers on every flat surface. A brocaded sofa and two fragile-looking armchairs cupped a low table in one corner, the wood dark and glossy from repeated waxing. The decor made the room look opulent, romantic and sexy in a warm hazy kind of way.

Roger was again assured that eventually he'd see a tip. Then he left, a small smirk on his lips that Alex caught and Thorn didn't as he was already standing on the balcony, his back to the room. Muted sounds of breaking surf came through the open doors.

Alex took a step toward him, then stopped. She hated to intrude, but she was suddenly so tired, she ached. She caught sight of herself in a mirror again and shook her head. The last time she'd faced her reflection she'd looked silly. Now she looked like a bride who had been dragged behind a car for a couple of miles. No wonder Candy had been so smug.

Thorn came through the doors, and Alex's overwhelming feeling was that it wasn't fair. He'd had an even worse day than she and yet he looked incredible. While it was true the emotions the man had been subjected to during the past twelve hours had sharpened the edges of his face and etched new lines around his eyes and mouth, it was also true that these very things somehow enhanced the sheer masculinity that seeped through his pores. For a few seconds he stared at her with a dark, brooding expression and she felt a quivering in her stomach.

"You look beat," he said.

Alex tried patting her hair back in place, but she knew that at this stage, it was pointless. "I am," she admitted.

"I am, too," he said. "Are you hungry?"

Maybe that was what had caused the uneasy feeling. "A little."

He nodded absently, sighed, and looked around the room. "There's only one bed," he said.

Alex smiled. "I noticed."

"You can have it. I'll take the sofa."

"Thorn, what are we going to do next?"

"I don't have the slightest idea."

As it was obvious he wasn't going to be able to make rational decisions until he got his feet back on the ground, Alex once again took charge. "Order us something to eat," she said, gesturing at the phone.

"I'm not hungry—"

"But you should have something to eat, and I'm suddenly ravenous. I'm going to take a bath." While he stood rooted to the floor, she closed herself in the bathroom. With some difficulty, she got the dress off, then the bulky truss. She stuffed the whole mess into a corner, which instantly reminded her of Natalie's wedding gown, abandoned on the closet floor.

Was the woman nuts? How could she walk away from a man like Thorn?

Alex shook her head. This wasn't any of her concern. This thing was between the two of them; she was just here as a disinterested third party.

She ran a deep bath of steaming water and lowered her body all the way under until only her nose broke the surface. Heaven. After washing her hair, she towel dried and faced herself in yet another mirror. That's when she realized she didn't have a comb or a toothbrush or a robe.

She just couldn't face the dress again. Maybe the hotel had robes hanging in the closet. She wrapped herself in a huge towel and knocked on the door.

"Thorn? Are you out there?"

No answer came.

She knocked louder and called his name again with the same results. Tentatively, she opened the door and stared into the empty room.

She crossed quickly to the closet and chuckled to herself when she found two thick white terry-cloth robes hanging side by side—his and hers, bride's and groom's. She plucked one off a hanger, darted back to the bathroom, replaced the towel with the robe and did her best to finger-comb her shoulder-length hair.

Thorn was still missing. Alex paced the floor and wondered what, if anything, she should do about it. What if he'd found Natalie and the two of them had kissed and made up and completely forgotten about her? How long should she hide out in the room?

A few minutes later, she answered a brisk knock on the door without asking who it was, flinging it wide open to find another man in another teal uniform, this one behind a covered cart.

"Room service," he said, rolling past her. Within a minute, he'd removed both the covers and himself, leaving Alex alone with a huge platter of cheese, a bowl of fruit, a basket of crackers, a chilled bottle of white wine and two glasses.

Did this mean Thorn was eventually coming back?

She nibbled on the food but ignored the wine. She'd never been much of a drinker—in fact, her sister teased her that she was a "cheap date," because she got giddy on the fumes alone. She wandered out to the balcony. The wind was cold and salty, and smelled like seaweed. The surf sounded distant—it must be low tide. She listened intently, wishing it was closer, louder, so that it would drown out her thoughts, because they kept circling back to her current role as Thorn's faithful sidekick. Truth of the matter was she suspected she didn't belong here, that she should put on her frilly dress and find a way home.

But not tonight, she told herself, shifting her gaze to the left. The curve of the building allowed her a view of the front of the inn where they had first arrived. In fact, she could make out Roger standing beneath one of the lights, which probably meant that the shaving cream previously decorating Thorn's car was now a thing of the past.

She wheeled around as a key rattled in the lock. The door opened and Thorn appeared. He looked defeated as he scanned the room with weary eyes, but Alex doubted the expression he wore had anything to do with concern for her whereabouts.

She closed the glass doors behind her. "You were out looking for Natalie, weren't you?" she asked as she poured him a glass of wine.

"Yes."

"Did you find her?"

He swallowed the contents with one long gulp. "No. If she's here, she's behind a closed door."

Alex looked down at the floor. She didn't need him to explain what he was imagining, what they were both imagining: Natalie wrapped in another man's arms, Natalie sharing another man's bed, while her groom stood rejected and alone.

Not alone, Alex amended internally. *I'm here.*

Chapter Three

Thorn's head hurt in a major way, as if a great big bull were tap dancing inside his skull. The sofa was too short and too narrow to offer much of a retreat. In fact, when he tried turning over, he came close to sliding off onto the floor. Head pounding, he gave up trying to sleep and sat on the edge of the cushion, listening for a moment to the barely perceptible sound of Alexandra's breathing.

This was not the way he'd imagined this particular night would pass, him on a sofa, a virtual stranger in his bed, and Natalie with some other guy.

Hell, this whole thing didn't even seem real. Real things were the fences he mended, especially the one running east to west near the stand of fir trees marking the southern border of his land. He liked throwing the lumber and tools into the back of his pickup, liked the bumpy road that crisscrossed through the cattle fields, liked finding a broken post or a sagging wire and fixing it. It was satisfying work, clear-cut, over and done with. And afterward, there was the shade of the trees, a perfect place for a cool drink and a well-earned lunch. Life reduced to basics, understandable, his to control.

Not like this. Not like wondering what the hell was happening to him, not like having his fate in someone else's hands. Damn Natalie! He would never let himself be this vulnerable again. Never.

He popped to his feet and paced for a few minutes. Five steps to the wall, five steps back, over and over again while his thoughts jumped around in his miserable brain.

He was suddenly flooded with memories of her. The first time he'd seen her in the flower shop, standing behind the counter, all smiles and green eyes with those beautiful strawberry curls surrounding her face. He'd needed flowers sent to his grandmother. He remembered how she'd insisted on showing him every photo in a book full of floral arrangements, how she had touched his arm with her hand when she spoke, and how, when he'd finally asked her to dinner, she had smiled up at him as though she knew something he didn't.

He remembered her in a bathing suit, all delicious curves and sun-warmed skin. She wouldn't go in his swimming pool, said something about chlorine and her suit, but when he'd suggested they go down to the pond, she'd laughed at him. Women were such mysteries to a man like him, such intricate mazes with twisty corridors and high walls, full of secrets.

Natalie in a sundress, Natalie in his lap, Natalie's eyes and her mouth and her perfect fingernails tapping against his arm. For four months there had been nothing and no one but Natalie, as if she'd cast some spell over him. *Well, never again,* he reminded himself. *Never, never again.*

He stopped pacing and crossed to the balcony doors, stopping on the way to look at Alexandra. Moonlight flooded her bed, kissing her face, so peaceful, in slumber. Her hair was fanned out on the pillow, surrounding her face like a soft, dark cloud. Natalie hadn't talked about this woman much. For that matter, she hadn't talked about any of her women friends. Why hadn't he noticed that before?

Alexandra. Such a long, fancy name for a woman so up-front and sweet, though she did seem to have a streak of humor that bubbled to the surface at odd times. She was sure being a good sport about all this, but he was ready to bet a bundle that come morning, she'd expect him to take her home. Maybe he'd just give her his keys and let her drive herself. At any rate, one thing was for certain—he wasn't leaving this place until he'd faced Natalie. He did not leave loose ends and right now, Natalie Dupree was one gigantic loose end.

Alexandra. On second thought, he liked the name. It fit her, for he sensed in her slight body a strong will and a fierce streak of independence that probably defined her to herself. The name was bold in a way, reminiscent of Alexander the Great. If memory served him right, old Alexander had been the king of Macedonia, the conqueror of the Persian empire. Tilting his head, Thorn stared at the face on the pillow before him, her soft and feminine features blurred by the moonlight.

The outside air was crisp and clean and did a lot to clear his head. As he leaned against the rail, he acknowledged the certainty he felt that Natalie was in this building. There was no real proof, of course. He'd tried looking for her car, but there were dozens of red compacts and he had no idea what her license number was. Tomorrow, he'd stake out the restaurants. If that didn't work, he'd start knocking on doors.

His headache all but disappeared as he stared up into the night sky. It was amazing that these ocean-hugging stars were the same ones he saw at home. For a second, he was back on the ranch, alone in the rambling house he'd built with his own two hands, out on the balcony that ran along the back of the house, gazing upward, picking out Orion and the Pleiades. He found these constellations now, smiling up at two old friends who didn't tell him that he should have known better, that he was a fool. "Thanks, guys," he whispered. "I appreciate it."

Alex awoke during the night, unsure what had called her back from a restless dream she could no longer remember. For a second, she lay beneath the satin quilt, placing herself in the honeymoon suite of the Otter Point Inn, alone in a huge bed meant for lovers.

Gradually she became aware of a cool breeze blowing in from the glass doors, and raised herself on her elbows to find long sheer curtains billowing back into the room, which meant the doors were open. The balcony was lit by the moon and she could just make out a dark shape standing at the rail.

An instinctive gasp died on her lips as she realized the shape was actually Thorn. His back was to her as he stared out at the sea.

He wouldn't throw himself down onto the rocks, would he?

No. As upset as he obviously was, he didn't act suicidal, just humiliated and angry. Now, if Natalie was here, that might be a different story. Natalie he might very well like to toss off a balcony.

Would he, or do I just want to believe he would?

This second question came from nowhere and left Alex feeling shaken.

She heard him close the doors as she slowly lowered her head back to the pillow and feigned sleep. His footsteps hardly made a sound on the plush carpet as he crossed back to the sofa. She heard the creak of old furniture as he lowered his weight and tried to get comfortable. He was paying for the room and she was half his size—why hadn't it occurred to her to take the sofa and let him have the bed?

Should she get up and offer the bed to him now? Would he want it? Maybe the sofa was a better place for a jilted bridegroom. She fell asleep again while trying to figure out what to do.

The next time she awoke, it was morning and sunlight streamed through the glass. As she got out of bed, Alex looked over at the sofa, half expecting to find Thorn gone again, but apparently his late-night reverie out on the balcony had taken its toll. He lay asleep, half on the sofa, one arm hanging off to the side, both feet dangling over the end. He'd kicked off the blanket she'd given him the night before and it lay in a heap on the floor. Thankfully, he at least slept in his underwear.

She stared at him longer than was strictly necessary. His hands and forearms were tanned the same deep color as his face, the rest of him a shade lighter. He had very nice legs, well shaped, muscular. She liked his ankles. He stirred and she turned away at once.

False alarm. When she dared to take another peek, he was sound asleep again, on his side, all arms and legs, his head half buried under an arm. Alex let herself out onto the balcony, anxious to escape Thorn.

The rocks below were black and jagged, the ocean that swirled around them, sapphire blue. For some time, Alex stared at the water. She was wearing the robe—indeed, she'd slept in the robe—and she tightened the belt around her waist. What was she going to put on this morning? Would Thorn have any clothes that would fit her? Maybe she could borrow his gold card and buy herself something in the gift shop—shorts and a T-shirt, a touristy dress printed with whales or dolphins. Anything!

She winced when she thought about the prices she knew she'd find. A confirmed bargain hunter, she tended to wait until clothing was marked down so far, it was a giveaway. Well, desperate situations called for desperate measures and all that.

As she turned to go back into the room, she caught sight of a small yellow sports car pulled up to the front of the inn. Then she realized what had really drawn her attention was the driver. He was a very tanned man with long white hair caught in a ponytail at the nape of his neck. He was facing the inn, a striking man in his fifties with eyes dark enough to stand out at a distance. He looked like the male lead in a spy movie.

She was about to turn away when a woman in a knee-length coat approached the passenger door of the car. The coat was an unusual shade, more orange than red, vibrant, eye-catching, hemmed in heavy black braid. A distinctive coat, a familiar coat, one Alex had seen every morning for the past six months. With a feeling of inevitability, her gaze traveled from the coat to a swirl of reddish-blond hair, and then, as the woman turned, to an upturned nose and a pair of huge dark glasses.

Alex raced back into the room, calling Thorn's name as she ran. By the time she got to the sofa, he was blinking the sleep from his eyes. She stood above him and pointed outside. "Natalie," she managed to say.

In a flash, he was on his feet and out the doors. She saw him peer over the railing, then back into the room toward her.

"Where?"

"Getting into a yellow car."

He looked over the railing. His expression as he faced Alex confirmed what she was afraid of.

"Too late?" she asked as she joined him.

"Apparently. Are you sure it was her?"

"Absolutely positive."

He nodded briskly. "Okay. Tell me what you saw while I get dressed."

Following him back into the room, she said, "There was a man in a yellow car."

He stopped dead in his tracks and turned again. "A man," he repeated woodenly.

"Yes. A much older man." She left out the part about

the way the man looked, the square set of his shoulders, his distinctive mane of hair. The man might be older than Thorn, but he was no slouch and he certainly didn't look like anyone's father. Of course, Thorn standing there only half-dressed didn't look like a slouch, either!

"Go on," Thorn said as he picked up his suitcase and threw it on the bed.

"In a second. I don't suppose there's anything in that suitcase I could wear?"

Thorn had grabbed the first clothes he came to—a white shirt and a pair of khaki slacks. With Alex's question, he turned to look at her, and for the first time, he seemed to notice she was in a robe, seemed to remember than she had no luggage. "I don't know, I'm a lot bigger than you are—"

"What about this?" Alex asked as she pulled a bright red-and-white Hawaiian shirt out of his bag.

"Sure, I don't care. Take anything you want. Just hurry."

As he dressed in the bathroom she described the rest of what she'd seen, her voice raised so he could hear through the wooden door. As she spoke, she put on the shirt and dug through his suitcase, emerging with a pair of baggy white swim trunks. They had a cord at the waist and she slipped them on, tightening the cord, then knotting the shirt. His shoes were impossibly big for her and she couldn't face the heels, so she decided to go barefoot.

By the time this was done, Thorn was out of the bathroom, completely dressed, looking like a million bucks. Again.

They opted for the stairs when the elevator took too long to answer the call. Thorn was at the desk before Alex. By the time she got there, the desk clerk was being grilled.

"Yes, I know who you are, Mr. Powell, and might I offer my heartfelt congratulations on your marriage."

This clerk was middle-aged with thinning black hair and

a clipped mustache. Alex had seen him watch her approach the desk in Thorn's wake. When she stopped beside Thorn, the clerk actually gave her a double take, as though he couldn't believe *the* Thorn Powell was hitched to this frizzy-haired woman swimming in men's clothes. Alex smiled pleasantly and said, "Good morning."

"Morning, ma'am," he said. His name was Alfred. To Alex, he looked like an Alfred. She couldn't imagine anyone calling him Alfie.

"Yes, yes," Thorn said. "I want to know about the woman who just left here. About five-eight, reddish hair, orange coat—"

"You mean Miss Blackwell," the clerk interrupted.

"Miss Blackwell?"

"Jasmine Blackwell. She's here with her father, Gerald Blackwell."

Alex leaned forward. "A man in his fifties with long white hair and black eyes?"

"Yes, that's him," the clerk said.

Thorn, his hands in tight fists, said, "How long have they been here?"

"Since yesterday afternoon," the desk clerk answered as he punched up the information on his screen.

"Did they arrive together or separately?"

Alfred gave a pained little smile and sighed. "Mr. Powell, I must assure you that I would not have answered even this many questions if it wasn't for the fact that you are such a valued guest and Mr. Hanks has left explicit instructions that we accommodate you in any way we can, but really, sir—"

"Together or apart?" Thorn repeated.

The desk clerk must have heard in Thorn's voice the same note of authority tinged with recklessness that Alex heard. He said, "Apart. Mr. Blackwell checked in several hours before Miss Blackwell."

Thorn stared at his feet. Alex knew he was reviewing facts in his mind. Then he said, "Where did they go?"

"Now, sir—"

The clerk slid Alex a loaded glance that clearly said, *This man is your husband. Get him off my back!* Alex smiled and shrugged.

"I'm sure I don't know," the clerk said at last.

"And I'm sure you do!" Thorn thundered.

Alex pulled on his arm. "Now, honey, this poor man is just doing his job, protecting the privacy of everyone, you know how it is. Remember when you got that other man fired, what was his name, Phil? Maybe it was Bill. Anyway, we don't want this man's job on our conscience now, do we?"

Thorn looked down at her and said, "Sure we do."

"To the airport," the clerk blurted out.

The answer surprised Alex and apparently Thorn, as well, for he stared at Alfred a full thirty seconds before demanding, "Why?"

"To catch a plane."

"Of course. But what plane and to where?"

Another moment of silence as the man thought about his options, threw Alex a glance more furtive than the previous one, then finally heaved a beleaguered sigh. "Miss Blackwell wanted to shop. I overheard them talking. They said something about Seattle."

"Have they checked out of the hotel?" Alex asked.

"No."

"Then they'll be back?" Thorn added.

The clerk nodded. "Mr. Blackwell said they would return this evening."

Alex mentally prepared herself for a day of lobby sitting, but Thorn took her arm. "Thanks, Alfred." He looked down at Alex and added, "Let's go get some breakfast."

Suddenly ravenous, Thorn ordered a big breakfast of steak and eggs, damn the cholesterol. He was a little surprised when Alexandra echoed his choice. She was smaller than 'Natalie and he'd expected her to eat the same way her friend did, which meant dry toast and tea for breakfast.

Once the food was consumed, he sat back in the leather armchair and stared out at the ocean, a second cup of coffee on the table in front of him.

"Thorn?"

He turned back to face Alexandra.

"I think I should go home," she said softly.

He leaned his arms on the table. "I can't drive you back now," he said. "I have to see this through."

"I know you do. But I don't belong here, and besides, I don't think you really need me hanging around."

He stared into her eyes and felt a stab of panic assail him at the thought of her leaving. "Yes, I do," he said. "You're Natalie's friend and you have to be here to keep me from throttling her."

"You're not going to throttle her," she said with a slow smile.

"Okay, I'm not going to throttle her. Still, I wish you'd reconsider. Besides, it'll be over tonight."

"But I work tomorrow—"

"I'll drive you home after we see Natalie."

She bit her bottom lip. "I don't know—"

"I'll make the wait worth your while," he said suddenly. This earned him another smile. "How?"

"We'll do something fun today. No reason we have to sit in the lobby when they won't be back until tonight."

She regarded him with her steady gaze that reminded him of the stars. "You're different this morning," she said.

"How?"

She shrugged. "I don't know. More lighthearted. Less...broken."

"Well, let's see. My fiancée is staying here under an assumed name with a man old enough to be her father, who may actually be her father—and if you believe that, I have a bridge to sell you. I spent yesterday in a daze, and tonight I'm going to hear her side of the story, but today, here I am at the beach with a pretty girl and a few hours to kill. Let me assure you that inside, I'm still shattered, enraged, perplexed and boondoggled, but damn, I'm tired of wallowing in it. Allow me this charming front.''

She laughed. ''Okay.''

''And stay with me, please.''

''As a distraction?'' she asked, her eyes now mocking.

''Yes,'' he admitted. ''Will you? You've come this far. Of course, if there's someone at home who will miss you, parents or friends you need to call, or pets to care for—''

''Nothing like that,'' she said, interrupting. ''I live alone, my parents are in Arizona and my only plans for today involved laundry. Okay, I'll see it through.''

''Good. Finish your steak, Alexandra, we have a lot to arrange.''

''I've eaten all I want.''

He nodded. For a man who should be feeling dumped and dismal, he felt remarkably good. Of course, a hearty breakfast always did wonders for his morale.

''There is one problem,'' Alex said. ''I don't have a comb or a toothbrush.''

He looked at her hair, *really* looked at it for the first time that morning, and grinned. She was a mess, all right. Of course, a few stray hairs didn't really detract from her face, but he could see that she needed some personal items.

''Then that's where we'll start,'' he told her.

They found a sundries store on the floor below the lobby and Thorn stood by as Alex picked out the three or four things she needed. He couldn't help but notice how modest her choices were or how often she told him she'd repay him. He tried telling her that she was there because of him, but in the end, he let it drop. If it made her feel better to repay him thirteen or fourteen dollars, then so be it.

He sent her up to the room by herself, then went back

to the lower-level shops and found one that sold women's clothing. There wasn't a whole lot to choose from, but as this was the only store he could shop at, he adapted to the limited selection.

Estimating her size, he chose a blue bathing suit with lots of little straps around the back. The only sweatshirt without a picture of some big-eyed animal plastered on the front was a bright purple one with pink sleeves, which he kind of liked. He grabbed a pair of red pants that looked as though they were made out of parachute material and should be cool or warm depending on the situation, then found the only sandals in the place—gold ones with flowers on the toes.

"Oh, Mr. Powell," the clerk told him as she rang up his purchases. "Are these things for the new Mrs. Powell?"

Thorn was bent over a rack, trying to decide what SPF the suntan lotion should be. He looked up at the clerk and said, "No."

"What!"

The woman's shocked voice roused him. He said, "What?" back at her.

"I asked if these items were for your new wife. The hotel grapevine, you know."

Oh, brother. "Ah—well, of course they are," he mumbled.

The woman, tight-lipped because she obviously didn't believe a word he said, wrapped his purchases in tissue paper, ran the hotel credit card through a machine and handed him the bag. "I'm sorry if I pried into your personal life," she said, her eyes downcast.

Great, Thorn thought. *Now the entire hotel will think I'm cheating on my wife of one day.* "You don't understand," he began, but then he dropped it. What was the use? When this was over, he'd just have to stay away from the Otter Point Inn for a while. But after the confrontation he envisioned with Natalie tonight, he doubted very much that he would want to come again anyway.

Back in the lobby, he cornered Alfred and arranged for a picnic and a couple of Boogie boards and wet suits to be delivered to his car. Then he took the elevator back to his room. Instinct told him what he needed was some sort of physical activity to make the time pass, to take his mind off what was to come. For a second he wondered if all his plans would blow up in his face—maybe Alex was as cautious about the water and the sun on her skin as Natalie was, but somehow he doubted it. Still, he'd skip the details until it was too late for her to back out.

Alex spent the time alone in the room to move her maid-of-honor dress and the truss to the empty closet where Thorn wouldn't have to constantly see them. She was just getting out of the shower when she heard a loud knock on the bathroom door. After wrapping herself in a towel, she opened it to find a blue sack in Thorn's outstretched hand.

"For you," he said. "Put the bathing suit on under your clothes. By the way, I looked in my suitcase but I can't find my suit. Were you wearing it this morning?"

His suit, which she'd used as shorts, was neatly folded and lying on the counter. "Yes," she said as she handed it back to him.

"Thanks."

"What's in the sack?" she asked as she opened it.

"Clothes and a bathing suit, like I said. I had to estimate your size. I hope everything fits."

"I can't accept—"

He cut her off. "Spare me all the protests, please. Just put on the clothes and let's get out of here."

She closed the door on him. "Where are we going?" she asked as she dumped out his clothes. What she needed was a pair of sunglasses—the clothes were all bright colors. Very bright colors. Damn near fluorescent! How could a man who dressed himself so well choose such strange clothes for someone else?

She heard him answer, but his voice was muffled and she guessed he'd moved off toward the glass doors and the balcony. At any rate, she didn't catch a single word. The bathing suit was a size too small, but she pulled it on anyway, a little confused at first as to where all the little straps were supposed to go. A bit tight in the bust, but not too bad. The other clothes were baggy, the sandals a size too big and a lot too fancy seeing as they were shiny gold with silver and black silk daisies glued to the toes. She tried pulling off the flowers but they were stuck on there for good. Resigned, she slipped them on and avoided her reflection.

"Oh, my," Thorn said, as she opened the door and he caught sight of her. "I guess I got a little carried away, didn't I? Well, you look nice in bright colors, Alexandra, and it seems as though everything fits. Kind of, anyway…"

He was wearing his swim trunks and a pair of rope sandals and nothing else. His chest was covered with a soft dusting of dark hair, which clung to his pectoral muscles and inflamed Alex with the incredible urge to touch him. He pulled on a knit shirt, which effectively saved the day.

"Are you okay?" he asked.

"All that steam made me dizzy," she mumbled as she fanned herself with an open hand.

"You okay now?"

"Fine."

"Are you sure?"

"Positive." She held up the suntan lotion. "Listen, Thorn, we're on the Oregon coast, where it's windy half the time and cold the other half. Why do we need bathing suits and this stuff?"

"Don't ask. It's a surprise."

"I hate surprises."

"Not really?"

"Yes, really."

He grinned at her. "Surely you can humor a jilted man?"

"You're not acting terribly jilted."

"Smiling through my tears."

She shook her head.

"I need to get away from here, Alexandra," he said, his voice suddenly serious. "I keep thinking about Natalie and the guy with the white hair. I need to get out in the open with the fresh air and the wind. If there were horses, I'd go riding, but there aren't. However, there is an ocean. Can't we just go?"

Instantly contrite, Alex gathered two towels from the bathroom and followed Thorn out of the room. Twice that morning, she'd assumed his banter was lighthearted; she hadn't considered the possibility that he was trying to make her feel comfortable or, perhaps more accurately, that he was hiding from the deep betrayal he must surely feel. She must stop calling him on it and just let him go. If he could have fun on a day like this, so could she.

Besides, she could hardly wait to see Alfred's expression when she appeared in the lobby wearing her latest getup.

Chapter Four

The beach Thorn drove to was three miles north of Otter Point. As they plodded across the dunes toward the water, Alex wondered how she'd manage on a Boogie board. Though she loved the outdoors, she wasn't an accomplished sportswoman and she'd never swum in the ocean before. The increasingly loud crash of the surf beckoned her forward, however, and she felt a certain pull toward the sea. Kind of like a lemming, she decided.

She followed in Thorn's wake. As his stride was twice what hers was, she used the downward side of the dune to try to catch up with him, for although he toted a majority of their paraphernalia, he left her in the proverbial dust when he climbed.

At last the dunes sloped down to a broad expanse of beach, a mile of sand dotted with rocks, and almost deserted. Thorn picked his way through the driftwood, breaking at last onto hard-packed sand, which was a lot easier to walk on. Alex was finally able to keep up with him, though in the deepest recess of her mind lurked the knowledge that she hadn't minded walking behind him, hadn't minded the view of his strong legs tensing and relaxing, not one bit.

"This is good," he said at last, dropping their belongings near an uprooted tree that had washed ashore sometime in the distant past. He immediately pulled off his shirt and stretched his arms upward. Sunlight spilled over his hair, shone on his face.

Alex used the time it took Thorn to pull on his wet suit to gather her wits. She folded and refolded towels, then sat on the log, averting her gaze.

"Aren't you coming?" he asked.

She looked up to find him standing in front of her, over six feet of male human swathed in burgundy rubber that molded his every contour. His eyes were the exact color of the beach, gray with sparkles, which mimicked the light-reflecting mica chips in the sand. The wind had run its chilly fingers through his hair, dumping it on his forehead, making him appear years younger.

"Of course," Alex said quickly. She scooted onto her feet and pulled off her sweatshirt. She couldn't help but notice that her breasts were spilling from the top of the suit, but as Thorn was watching her, she tried to ignore them. She realized she should have used the time he took to tug on his wet suit to do the same so that he wouldn't now be idle with nothing to do but look at her struggling with her clothes.

"Have you ever worn a wet suit before?" he asked.

"Ah, no." She picked up the wet suit, treating the poor man to heaven-knew-what view as she leaned down. She put one foot in the rubberlike material and wondered how on earth she was going to get into the thing.

"Sit down on this log," Thorn said, pointing to the tree. She sat as directed.

He knelt in front of her and together, they got the suit on over her feet, up her legs, past her hips. "I'll take it from here," she told him as she stood and slipped both her arms into the suit and pulled it up over her chest. The zipper was in the back, and Thorn reached around her, tugging on the pull until it closed up near the nape of her neck.

He checked her over with the dispassionate gaze of a parent making sure his kid has on the proper rain gear before walking to school in a storm. "Are you warm now?"

"Yes." Alex knew he was staring at her. She wondered what she looked like in the bright pink and yellow wet suit that hugged her every bump and dip the same way Thorn's hugged his. She knew he wouldn't be thinking about her in exactly the same way she was thinking about him, wouldn't be noticing things like the color of her eyes or the shape of her body, because his mind was on Natalie. Of course, it was on Natalie.

He glanced down at their belongings. "Where's the sunscreen?"

Chuckling, Alex said, "We're both covered from neck to ankle. Where would we put sunscreen?"

He touched the tip of her nose. "Right here."

They found the sunscreen. "Allow me," he said, as he squeezed a little onto his fingertips and dabbed Alex's nose. The stuff smelled like coconut oil. His fingers moved across her cheeks, caressed her ears, ran down her neck. Alex closed her eyes and his touch was almost that of a lover.

"That should do you," he said.

She opened her eyes. He was rubbing sunscreen on his own face. She wanted to offer to return the favor by helping him, but she didn't trust her fingers not to linger over his features and give her true feelings away.

And what are my true feelings? she asked herself. *Sympathy? Ha, more like plain old unadulterated lust! Come off it, girl, slow down.*

"Are you ready to get in the water?"

"Sure." She took the short fiberglass board Thorn handed her, strapping a Velcro tether around her wrist as he did. "We look like a couple of surfer dudes," she said.

"A surfer dude and a surfer dudette." He chuckled. Looking past her shoulder, he added, "Do you remember what I told you about Boogie boarding while we were driving here?"

"Of course. Take the board out into the water, wait for a big wave to threaten your life, fling yourself on top of it."

That snapped his gaze back to her face. With a somewhat alarmed expression, he mumbled, "Well, that's it, more or less. Just remember to hold on to the handles that are molded into the nose of the board."

The cold water stung her feet as she followed Thorn into the ocean. The brief thought flickered across her mind that she was always following him somewhere. The thought was discarded as the water reached her groin, and wet suit or no wet suit, she felt a cold chill travel through her body. Mercifully, it was quickly replaced by numbness.

Thorn caught a wave almost at once, disappearing toward land in a thunderous wash of bubbling water, gliding almost onto the sandy beach as the water receded. Alex watched him get to his feet, thrust the board under one powerful arm and jog back toward her. His face was lit with a grin; he looked like a kid to Alex. As a matter of fact, someday he'd have children, and they'd look just like him when their cares were washed away.

She attempted to catch a wave, but her upper-body strength was nothing to write home about and it slipped away beneath her. Thorn was constantly in motion, either kicking to catch a wave or riding the top of it to the beach. Alex watched him to try to learn technique because she was determined to make a success out of this adventure. She'd just missed another ride when Thorn's voice came from behind her.

"Let me help you." Before she could respond, strong hands gripped her around the waist and slid her up on the board. "I'll push, you kick like mad," he added.

She glanced back at him. He was looking over his shoulder, gauging the wave action, waiting for the perfect opportunity to help launch Alex on her first ride. Meanwhile, one hand was on her board, and the other was tightly gripping her left calf. His own board floated slightly behind them, connected to Thorn by the tether.

Alex felt his hand stiffen and then she saw the wave. It was twice as big as anything she'd so far seen, a huge green monster building in power and size as it raced across the ever-shallowing ocean floor.

"Yikes," she squealed.

"Maybe it's too big for you," Thorn said.

"It's just right," she told him with more bravado than she felt.

"Alexandra—"

The wave was upon them. Alex kicked with all her might. She couldn't tell if Thorn pushed her or not; she had the feeling he didn't need to. A rush of adrenaline hit her like a freight train as the board took flight, a ton of angry water beneath her, the beach approaching at a frightening speed. Alex held on to the handles so tight, her knuckles ached.

For thirty seconds or so, she flew, she was free, she was a winged creature skimming the sea. And then the board suddenly flipped over, her with it, and the world became a swirling whirlpool of saltwater, sand and sky, none of it where it belonged, all of it one and the same.

She wasn't sure which direction was which, just that the board was gone, which was a relief as it had acted like an anchor, yanking her this way and that. But even without the board, she continued being thrown about like a small load of laundry in a maniacal washing machine. She hit the sandy floor on her shoulder. She was lifted and thrown again and this time she landed on her left wrist and it bent painfully beneath her body in a way that a wrist was not intended to bend. Instantly, she was tossed toward the surface—was it the surface?—and back again, landing on her hip, jarred and shaken, sand in her eyes and nose, panic one blink away.

Someone grasped her around the torso and lifted her. One hand slid down her body, cupping her behind the knees, hefting her into the air. She narrowly opened her eyes to find Thorn gazing down at her.

He carried her toward the beach. "My God, are you okay?"

"I—I lost the Boogie board," she stammered.

"It doesn't matter. How about you?"

She thought to herself that she should insist he put her down, that she could easily walk on her own, but instead she nodded and closed her eyes. There was such a feeling of safety in his arms with his chest so hard beneath the cushiony layer of wet suit. She could hear his heart pounding. Or was the sound the surf? Or was it her own heart?

He knelt on the sand and laid her down. "Alexandra?"

His arms were gone. She was alone again and the pounding noise remained. It was her own heart, beating like a drum. How long could a heart beat like that before it broke free of the ribs and burst from the chest?

"Alexandra!" he repeated.

She opened her eyes again. Pretty little white clouds floated above her head. She looked out at the ocean and was startled to find it peaceful and innocent.

"Are you okay?"

She scooted slightly into a sitting position, wincing with pain as her left wrist bore her weight.

Thorn immediately caught her hand and she gasped. He released her at once. "Is it broken?"

She tried moving it. "I...I...don't think so," she said, her voice dazed.

"I'm so sorry," he said. "I saw that wave coming and I knew it was too much for you but it was too late—"

"It's okay, it's okay," she said as she spit sand out of her mouth.

"I should never have encouraged you to go out there."

She frowned. "Accidents happen, Thorn. Besides, the ride I got before all hell broke loose was almost worth the crash."

He sat back on his heels and stared at her, his expression puzzled or incredulous, Alex wasn't sure which. "We'd better get you to a doctor—"

"No. My wrist is just twisted. It doesn't hurt much."

"Your face says it hurts a lot," he insisted.

"My face is an awful liar. I've had trouble with it before."

"And you have a scratch up by your eye. You're bleeding a little—"

"It's nothing," she said again, grabbing a dry towel with her good hand, dabbing at her face with the soft terry.

He obviously didn't believe her. Ignoring her protests, he dug through the picnic hamper and found a bottle of fresh water, which he used to wash the sand out of Alex's eyes and gently dab her scrapes. Then he stared at her again. "You don't look too bad," he said slowly.

"Gee, thanks."

"Still, we'd better go."

"We just got here. Is that my Boogie board over there?"

Thorn looked down the beach to where she pointed. "I'll get it," he said, and jogged away to retrieve the bright blue board from the surf a hundred yards down the beach. Alex used the time he was gone to check out her wrist, which was definitely hurt but not broken and to tug the picnic basket closer.

He dropped her board next to his. "What are you doing?"

"Is there food in this thing, too?"

"Food?"

"I'm hungry," she said, quietly holding her left hand in her right hand.

He stared at her a moment longer. Alex wondered why he did that so much. Was she so hard to understand that he had to continually review what she'd said or done?

"There's food in the basket," he said at last.

"Great. I'll sit here like the Queen of Sheba and you serve me, okay?"

"But a doctor—"

"No," she said firmly. Smiling, she added, "I'm thirsty, too, Thorn. I hope there's some more water in there."

Thorn shook his head, but he opened the basket and withdrew a couple of chilled bottles of ice tea. "This will have to do," he said as he handed her one.

She watched him swallow his, dropping her gaze when he caught her looking at him.

"Don't you like ice tea?"

She blurted out, "What?"

"You're not drinking. I thought you were thirsty."

Alex downed the tea and stared out at the benign waves while Thorn produced the rest of the meal. They ate avocado and black olive sandwiches on thick slabs of herb bread, the ocean and the few gulls overhead providing alfresco music. Alex didn't know what thoughts occupied Thorn; she only knew hers were becoming increasingly centered on him. She was aware, too aware, of how he looked when he took a bite and chewed it, how his expression changed when he looked out at the sea, how his hair fluttered in the wind as he moved his head. Her feelings were inappropriate, she knew this. The man was on a quest; she was along as solace or support or something or other. She had to get her thoughts in order.

And yet he seemed so happy and content today. Could part of that have anything to do with her, or was it all just an act?

"That was delicious," she said as he began packing away the leftovers.

"They have a wonderful kitchen staff at that place. Did you get enough?"

"Plenty."

His hand emerged with a covered plastic container. "Looks like there's dessert," he said, untaping the two forks that were attached to the lid.

"I'm a sucker for sweets," Alex said. "My sister says I could live on them."

"You have a sister? Older or younger?"

"Older. She had her first baby five days ago."

"Congratulations, Aunt Alexandra. Where does your sister live?"

"In Tacoma, Washington."

"And your parents live in Arizona?"

"Right, near Tucson. Dad is into deserts now, so their yard looks like a botanical exhibit, heavy on the cactus. Mom just likes to bake in the sun and court skin damage. How about you? Brothers and sisters?"

"One sister, two years younger."

"Does she live near you or with your parents—"

"My parents had their own spread adjacent to mine but they retired a few years ago, told me to watch the home front and joined United Hearts."

"Which is…?"

"It's a Peace Corps type of thing, except they rely on older, more experienced people like my folks."

Alex smiled. "You must be very proud of them."

"You bet." He stared down at the sand a moment, and then cast Alex a stern frown. "They're both at the house right this minute. They traveled here all the way from Central America to be at my wedding."

Alex, feeling a little inadequate to comment on this man's life, mumbled, "I'm sure they understand—"

"Yeah. Well, at least they have Linda to visit. Linda—

that's my sister—came down from Canada with her husband and her three little boys. You'd like Linda—she's a real gardener. That woman has a way with plants and flowers and stuff. Like you."

"And how do you know I have a way with plants and flowers and stuff?" she asked, genuinely curious.

"I've seen you in the shop, I've seen the fancy way you arrange the flowers. I even bought a teacup full of tiny roses that someone said you did. It was for the wife of one of my hands, and she'd just given birth to twin girls. She loved it, by the way."

The fact that he'd actually noticed her stunned Alex. It pleased her, too. *Fool,* the little voice deep inside whispered. She said, "I have to admit I love my job. Not everyone is so lucky."

He nodded. "I feel the same way about the ranch. The land, the animals, the trees…they're all a part of me."

Their eyes met again. At last Alex gestured at the container. "Aren't you going to open it?"

He flashed her a smile. "You really are fond of sweets."

"I really am."

The smile deepened. "So am I," he said, and for just a second, it was as though the words had a double meaning. Alex felt her heart race as once again those gray eyes dove into hers.

He turned his attention back to the container. All hints of a smile faded as the lid came off and they both realized what dessert consisted of. Inside the container, nestled in a paper doily, was a fancy square of frosted cake, white, with two silver hearts intertwined. One heart had Thorn's name in the middle, and the other had Alexandra's.

Natalie, who had hovered in the recesses of both of their minds, now squatted in the middle of the picnic.

"Wedding cake," he said, his voice wooden.

"They think—"

"I know." He snapped the lid back on the container.

When he finally met Alex's eyes, his expression was remote. "I'm not really hungry for sweets after all," he said.

"Neither am I," she told him.

Thorn closed the hotel room door behind him and stood, back against the hallway wall, idly looking at his feet. Inside the room, Alexandra was getting a once-over from the hotel doctor. She wasn't happy about it, but he'd insisted.

Sighing heavily, he glanced at his watch and saw that it was pushing evening. The hours were racing onward, toward the time Natalie and Gerald Blackwell would enter the lobby. He tried to imagine what would happen, how she'd look, what she'd say. Harder to imagine is what he'd feel when he saw her. Empty? Devastated? Heartsick?

She'd taken his future when she'd left. Without a backward glance, she'd wrapped up all the promises she'd made and shipped them to the end of the earth. Gone were the children they'd planned. Okay, okay, *he'd* planned. She hadn't been interested in a family. She'd wanted to travel; she'd been so full of plans for all the places they would see and all the things they would do. All that was gone.

He sighed again. Another glance at the watch showed him that he'd been thinking about Natalie for fifteen minutes. That meant the damn woman had stolen another chunk of his life.

The door opened and a middle-aged woman wearing a red suit and carrying a black doctor's bag stepped into the hall. She treated him to a professional smile.

"Your wife is just fine, Mr. Powell."

Thorn nodded. This whole subterfuge of Alexandra being his wife was wearing thin, yet he was powerless to stop it now. "Thank heavens," he said. He didn't have to pretend to be relieved about that.

"She's sprained her wrist, that's all. I've given her a mild painkiller and suggested she see her own doctor after you return from your honeymoon."

"Her own doctor," he snapped. "Why? What's wrong—"

"Nothing, nothing," she assured him, and then with a hint of laughter in her voice, added, "You newlyweds. Please, don't be alarmed, she's going to be fine. I only want her to check in with her doctor as a safety precaution."

"Oh, I see," he said.

"And, of course, she'll have to be careful for a few days while it heals."

"Of course."

"So you just continue to spoil her and don't let this accident wreck your honeymoon." She tilted her head and added, "Are you okay?"

"Me?"

"You seem a little on edge."

"I haven't been sleeping much—"

He stopped talking when her gaze dropped to her hands. He knew what she was thinking, that he was sleep deprived because of endless hours of lovemaking with his new wife. "I'm fine," he added.

The doctor nodded and briskly walked down the hall toward the elevator. Thorn reentered the room.

Alexandra was propped up in bed, staring out the windows. She turned to face him as he walked toward her, her dusky blue eyes echoing the smile that turned up the corners of her mouth.

"Still mad at me for insisting on a doctor?" he asked, standing above her.

She shook her head. She'd showered once they returned from the beach, and was now tucked into a fluffy white robe. Unbidden, the memory of her in the skimpy blue bathing suit flashed across his mind—the tiny straps crisscrossing her back, the top of the suit, which she filled to overflowing, the rounded curve of her backside, the blue fabric stretched taut over her flesh.

These thoughts fled as he spied her left wrist, which was

wrapped in an elastic bandage. She held it gingerly with her right hand as though supporting it.

"Here," he said, removing a small pillow from the sofa and laying it beside her. "Maybe you can prop your hand on this."

"Thanks."

He glanced at his watch again.

Alexandra cleared her throat. "You'd better go on down to the lobby."

"No, I couldn't leave you—"

"I'm fine. A little tired, in fact. You go on down and wait for Natalie and Gerald Blackwell to return. I'll join you later."

"I wouldn't feel right—"

She interrupted him again. "The only reason we're here is so that you can confront Natalie. Please, don't worry about me. Just go and do it. I'm going to take a nap. We still have a long drive ahead of us tonight."

She closed her eyes as if to punctuate her sentences and seal her intentions. Thorn felt odd about leaving her and yet she did have a point.

"You'll have them page me if you need anything?"

"Yes," she told him, opening her eyes again. "I'll be fine." Her hair was still wet, black and shiny, combed straight back from her forehead. Despite the sunscreen, her nose was sunburned, and the small scratches next to her eye looked moist, as though the doctor had treated them with antibiotic ointment.

Thorn admired her composure, and yet he wasn't surprised by it. All that day she'd startled him with her humor and her factual way of looking at things, with her lack of hysteria and her unflagging good spirits. He realized with a start that he *liked* this woman, that he even admired her!

"There's room service—"

"I know, Thorn. Don't worry about me, just go."

He left.

                          * * *

Alex awoke sometime later. It had been light outside when she'd drifted off to sleep but the sun had set some time ago and the room was now dark. Her left wrist throbbed, but the pain wasn't unbearable. Maybe that was due to the pill the doctor had given her.

She rolled over carefully and switched on the bedside lamp. The clock revealed it was almost midnight. She got out of bed and walked to the center of the room, a little lightheaded, a little hungry. For some time she stood there, uncertain what to do.

Had Natalie returned to the hotel? Had Thorn confronted her? Was he sitting down there all alone, broken-up inside? Was he celebrating his independence in the bar or had they found a way to mend their fences, so to say. Were they together now?

For thirty minutes, she paced between the balcony and the sofa, and then, unable to bear the suspense a second longer, she picked up the telephone and dialed the lobby.

"Front desk" came the quick response. It sounded like the woman from the night before. Candy, that was her name.

"Hello," Alex said. "This is Al...Mrs. Powell up in the honeymoon suite. Is Thorn...is Mr. Powell down there?"

"Why, yes, he is," Candy said. "He's been sitting down here for hours." There was a note of speculation in her voice. Of course, she'd be curious why a newlywed man would spend an evening camped out in the hotel lobby.

"He's...waiting for someone," Alex explained.

"I wouldn't know anything about that, Mrs. Powell," Candy replied.

Regretting her impulse to call, Alex hung up the receiver. She threw on the clothes she'd worn to the beach and made her way downstairs.

At this time of night, the lobby was dimly lit. Soft laughter and even softer music floated through the door of the lounge, which was off to the left. Clusters of chairs and love seats were almost empty except for a navy blue set that faced the doors.

Thorn sat alone, his head bent. Alex approached him slowly, not knowing if he was awake or asleep or miserable or anxious.

"Thorn?"

He glanced up at once. His eyes widened when he saw her and he stood. "Alexandra? Are you okay?"

She saw that his focus was on her wrapped wrist. "I'm fine. How about you?"

"Oh, I'm dandy, just dandy," he said, his voice sarcastic.

"Did you see Natalie? Did you speak with her?"

"Neither. She never showed up."

Alex sank down on the couch. "Oh." The fact of the matter was that it had never occurred to her that Natalie wouldn't come, that this night would stretch on the way the day had, that this thing might never have a resolution.

He sat back down beside her.

"It's only twelve forty-five," Alex said after glancing at the clock behind the counter.

"I called the airport," Thorn said. "Natalie and her...friend...were in a private plane. Did she ever say anything to you about her father having a pilot's license?"

"No."

"Me neither. As if I could still believe she's off with her father."

Alex didn't respond because she agreed with him. Instead, she touched his arm. "Have you eaten anything tonight?"

"The desk clerk brought me a cup of coffee an hour ago."

"Stay here," she told him, and getting to her feet, crossed the lobby to the lounge. The bartender smiled at her as she approached. Well, no wonder. The crazy clothes she wore were now sandy and wrinkled to boot. And then she wondered if he was just being polite and she was getting paranoid.

Using Thorn's name and the promise of a huge tip, she convinced him to carry two bottles of soda and a giant basket of pretzels back to the lobby. For another two hours, she and Thorn sat on the sofa, nursing their drinks, crunching their salty dinner, saying very little, each minute dragging its feet as though reluctant to relinquish its hold.

A heavy sigh from Thorn jolted Alex from near sleep and she glanced up at the clock behind the desk. It was almost 3:00 a.m.

"It's time to go up to our room," Thorn said. "We might as well go to sleep and face this tomorrow."

Alex nodded. She had no intention of staying at this hotel another day, but tomorrow morning would be soon enough to talk about it. Not even tomorrow, she realized groggily. Daybreak was only a few short hours away.

"Tomorrow I'll coerce Alfred into telling me Blackwell's room number," Thorn said as he stood. He offered Alex a hand and pulled her to her feet.

"Poor Alfred," she muttered.

Upstairs in the room, they took turns using the bathroom, then Thorn looked at the sofa.

"I'll take it tonight," Alex said.

"Not with your wrist all banged up."

She looked at him. "We both need a decent night's rest."

He shrugged. Wrapped in one of the hotel robes, his tanned face stark against the white cloth, he looked several steps beyond tired.

"We'll both sleep on the bed."

He looked relieved but said, "Are you sure?"

"Yes. It's a huge old thing. I'll get under the covers, you sleep on top. Grab your blanket—"

"But Alexandra, really, I wouldn't feel right—"

"I'm way too tired to argue with you," she said as she got under the covers.

She was very aware of him as he took the blanket from the couch and crossed the room to the other side of the bed. With his back to her, he took off the robe and though she fully intended on looking away, she found her gaze mesmerized as the heavy garment fell to the floor. He was wearing nothing but silk boxer shorts. His bare back was broad and well muscled and extremely provocative.

He turned off the lamp and lay back on the bed. She felt the mattress shift as he got comfortable, heard the rustle of his clothes and skin against the satin bedspread.

"Are you warm enough?" Her voice sounded small in the dark room.

"I'm fine," he said.

"I want to thank you, Thorn. For rescuing me today, I mean. And getting the doctor to come up here. It was very kind of you."

"You want to thank me?" he said, clearly amused.

"What's the matter?"

"Let's see, here you are with no decent clothing, eating pretzels for dinner, your hand all messed up, all because of me, and you're the one saying, 'Thanks'?"

"Well, when you put it that way—"

"I'm the thankful one, Alexandra. You've been very patient."

"You're most welcome." She closed her eyes, but sleep was elusive. Eventually, she opened them again and discovered she'd acquired a little night vision. Thanks to the moonlight that flooded the balcony and spilled through the glass doors, she found she could make out Thorn's profile. She was surprised to see a reflected gleam in the whites of his eyes, which meant he was still awake, too.

"Can't sleep?"

"You neither?"

She sighed. "Maybe I'm too tired."

"I know the feeling."

She doubted it. The fact of the matter was that the very proximity of this man was disturbing. Heat from his body radiated through the blankets. His breathing was deep and sensual. She was aching to have the privilege to touch his face, to fold herself into his arms. The intensity of these desires was all the more startling for, less than forty-eight hours before, she'd thought of Thorn only in the context of being Natalie's fiancé.

Not true, not true, an inner voice protested. *You've been thinking about him for weeks, and in ways a maid of honor should never think about a friend's man.* She recalled the way he had sometimes come into the shop dressed in work clothes, dusty boots and a much-worn black Stetson, his expression betraying how out of place he felt in primarily a woman's domain, how his eyes would light up when Natalie appeared and hurried him away.

"I wonder where *she* is," Thorn said.

His voice was soft, drowsy. Alex felt a stinging sensation behind her nose. She turned over on her side so that she wasn't facing Thorn and made a noncommittal sound, which she hoped he would interpret as meaning that she was just too tired to talk about Natalie Dupree.

"She must have stayed in Seattle," he said around a yawn.

Alex kept quiet.

"With *him,*" he added. "I wonder what he has that I don't. Tell me what he looked like, Alexandra. Details, I mean."

She kept her eyes and mouth shut. She didn't want to talk about Gerald Blackwell, either.

"Ah, it doesn't really matter," he mumbled, his voice increasingly faint. A long pause roused the hope in Alexandra's heart that he'd fallen asleep, but then he continued. "Did you ever notice her eyes, I mean *really* notice them? They're deep, deep green, like well water, eyes that look right into a man's soul and turn his insides to mush. She had me coming and going and I knew it and I didn't care. Have you ever felt like that about someone, Alexandra?''

Alex bit her lip. Natalie had cast a spell over this guy, and no matter what his rational mind thought, he was still affected.

''I guess you haven't, or you'd be in his bed and not here,'' he said, obviously thinking she was asleep.

I am in his bed! her heart screamed.

''Well, no matter,'' he said, his voice now so soft, Alex had to stop breathing so she wouldn't miss what he said. ''It's all flimflam, you know. Smoke and mirrors, nothing real. But I'll tell you one thing. I'll never give my heart to another woman. I won't go through this again. Never again.''

Alex buried her face in her pillow. She knew he'd get over Natalie, but then, eventually, he'd fall for another woman just like her because, in his heart of hearts, that's what he believed a woman should be. She, Alexandra Williams, would never be able to work magic on this man the way Natalie had because she lacked the cunning and guile—to say nothing of the desire—to manipulate him.

The bed creaked as he turned over.

Alex stared into the dark room, his words echoing in her head. *Never again...*

Chapter Five

A thump on the bed snapped Alex awake. As she sat up, she noticed three things at once: her wrist ached, the bedside clock said it was 11:00 a.m. and Thorn was throwing things into his suitcase, which he'd flung onto his side of the bed.

He stared at her for a few seconds with eyes that mirrored her own fatigue. She knew he'd tossed and turned the night away because she'd been awake, too, listening to him. She didn't think either one of them had had more than two or three hours of sleep.

"You have a black eye," he said. "Damn, I'm sorry."

Alex's hand flew to her face, where she gingerly touched the scrapes from the day before. "A shiner?"

"A beaut."

"It's my first one," she told him as she hopped from the bed.

"'Jasmine' and Gerald Blackwell didn't come back to the hotel," he said as she peered at herself in the mirror over the dresser.

The black eye, which really wasn't that bad, was easy to

turn away from. Alex perched on the edge of the dresser, her left wrist held up to reduce the throbbing and said, "How do you know?"

"I put the fear of God into Alfred, our friendly desk clerk. He finally told me they called very late last night and asked that their suitcases be flown to Seattle. The bags are already gone, but I got the name of the hotel they're staying in. A place called the Red Swan."

"A very ritzy joint," Alex said. She was beginning to realize that this was where she and Thorn went their separate ways, and the feeling this thought produced in her stomach was unsettling. She cinched the robe tighter around her waist, which wasn't easy as she had only one good hand.

"How do you know? Have you stayed there?" he asked as he crammed his tuxedo into the case. A pair of shiny black shoes followed.

"I had a drink there with Vicky—that's my sister—before she got pregnant. Two drinks cost us twenty-five dollars."

"Well," Thorn said, his voice as dry as an Arizona drought, "we all know our Natalie likes to hang out with money."

Alex looked down at her bare feet. How could Natalie have had this man so taken with her that he was willing to marry her, give her his name, share his future with her—and then just leave him, apparently for someone with more money than he had? Jeez, how much money did a person need? It was beyond her comprehension that anyone could have Thorn Powell and not want him.

"So we're off to Seattle," he said.

This comment snapped Alex from her thoughts. "Seattle?"

"Sure. You don't think I'm going to quit now, do you?"

She stared at him for a long count of thirty before answering. "Shouldn't you?"

"Hell, no, I shouldn't!"

"But you have people waiting for you at the ranch. Your parents and your sister and her family—"

"I called there this morning, just to see, you know, if maybe Natalie had left a message. Of course, she hadn't, but I did get to speak with everyone and explain what I'm up to. They all have plans of their own. Remember, as of yesterday, I was supposed to be away on my honeymoon, so no one built their trip around my being there." He glanced quickly around the room, and added, "What do you want to do about your dress? It's too big to fit inside my suitcase, but I could call the shop and have them send up another—"

"Wait a second," she interrupted.

He glanced at his watch and then at her. "You should get dressed before room service shows up with a pot of coffee and some bagels—"

"I'm not going to Seattle," she said.

He looked totally dumbfounded. "What? Why not?"

"Because this is your quest, not mine. I'm a working girl, remember? That reminds me, I'm already late for work. Crystal Caruthers will have a cow."

"No, you're not," he said.

She grabbed the phone with her good hand. "No, I'm not what?"

"Late for work. I called the shop and explained you'd sprained your wrist. Ms. Caruthers said for you to take the week off, that she would call someone named Sally who would cover for you. She said it was about time you took some of your sick leave."

Alex recradled the receiver and stared at Thorn's innocent expression before erupting. "You had absolutely no right to do that!"

"Look at the way you're holding your arm," he countered. "You can't work when you're hurt."

"Maybe not, but it wasn't your place to call my boss. I should have done that."

"You were asleep."

"You could have woken me."

"Yes, I suppose I could have but it seemed to me you had a restless night. Okay, I'm sorry. I shouldn't have interfered in your job."

"No, you shouldn't have. Has it ever occurred to you that I may have a life, too, that I don't have the time or the desire to run off with you on this crazy search, that other people might depend on me or worry about me if I disappear?"

He stared hard at her before answering. "Of course it has. Didn't I ask you yesterday if there were people you needed to call—"

"Yesterday was a Sunday. Today is a workday. I should be at work."

"You can't work—"

"I know I can't work."

"Then what are we arguing about?"

"We're arguing about your assuming you can run my life like you run your ranch."

"I'm not trying to run your life," he snarled. "I only wanted to make things easier for you."

"Well, don't do it again."

"Trust me, I won't."

"Good."

"Now hurry and get dressed—"

"I'm not going to Seattle, Thorn. This is where I get off."

"You're still mad that I called the flower shop!"

"No. It's just that it's time for me to go home."

"How are you going to get there?" he asked pleasantly as he snapped the suitcase shut and put it on the floor.

Obviously he wasn't going to drive her. She said, "I don't know. I'll find a way."

Thorn came around the bed, grabbed a straight-backed chair from the desk and set it down backward in front of Alex. He sat down on it, his arms over the top rung, facing her. "Please," he said, touching her hand, "stay with me, Alexandra."

"Don't waste your charm on me," she told him, smiling despite herself.

"Come on now. Don't you want to finish this? Don't you want to see Natalie's face when she realizes we've hunted her down?"

"No."

"Then do it for me," he said, the playful banter of a moment ago gone from his voice.

She could feel herself weakening. "Why should I?"

"Because you like me."

She swallowed painfully. Had her emotions showed that clearly? Instantly she felt her cheeks grow warm, and she dropped her eyes. He continued as though completely unaware how his words had affected her.

"I've never had a female friend before," he said. "I've had lovers and almost a wife, but never a friend, I mean, not one who was a woman. It's a new feeling for me and I kind of like it. I got the feeling you cared about me, too, in just the same way, as a friend."

"You're using me," she said softly.

"You bet I am. And I'll pay you back, you know. I'll nurse you back to good health. Look, Alexandra, just think of this next leg of the trip as an all-expense-paid minivacation to the beautiful state of Washington."

She smiled as she once again met his gaze. "How are you going to accomplish that?"

"What?"

"The 'all-expense-paid' part. Once you leave this place, you return to being a man without a wallet."

"The hotel will pack us another lunch, so that takes care of food and I know a guy in Portland who will lend me enough money to buy a tank of gas. I'll call the ranch and arrange to have my wallet sent overnight express mail to the hotel in Seattle, the what do you call it, the Red Swan.''

Alex stared at him, biting her lip, thinking. So, she was his first female friend. Not exactly the title she yearned for, but maybe it was a start. This was crazy. She should bail out now while she could.

I'll never give my heart to another woman, he'd said with meaning.

"How about it?"

Alex stared into his eyes. She heard herself say, "My sister lives about thirty miles this side of Seattle. Have it sent to her house and you can arrive at the hotel all prepared for battle."

A wide smile cracked his handsome face. "Does this mean you're going with me?"

"I haven't seen my new niece yet, and a call or two to Cottage Grove to cancel a couple of engagements ought to clear the next few days. Okay, I'll go with you to Seattle, but no farther."

He grinned. "Make your calls—"

"You first."

He took the phone from her lap and dialed. As it rang on the other end of the line, he said, "You watch. By this time tomorrow, it'll all be over."

"Where have I heard that before?" she mumbled.

It was another beautiful coastal day, clear and cool, the ocean a deep blue off to the left of the car as they drove north. After twenty or so miles, they turned east and began moving inland. The temperature climbed.

Alex had looked through her limited wardrobe and reluctantly put back on the sweatshirt and the parachute pants. They were too hot for the day but other than the bathing suit and bridesmaid dress, which was stuffed into a corner of Thorn's trunk along with the umbrella and the tin-can streamers, she didn't have much choice. She thought longingly of her sister's closet, of all the jeans and shorts and T-shirts a person could want. And underwear. And shoes that fit. And a blow dryer for her hair. And mascara. And lipstick.

"We may have to push this car to Portland," he said, jarring her from her thoughts.

She glanced at the fuel gauge. From her angle in the passenger's seat, it looked as though they must be running on fumes. "With our luck, we probably will."

"She used to say that," Thorn said softly.

No question to which "she" he referred, not when his voice took on that tone.

"Only, the other way around," he continued. "She used to say we had good luck, that nothing bad ever happened to us."

"Well, since I've been around, your luck seems to have taken a decided turn for the worse," Alex said.

"Yeah."

She didn't like the way he agreed so readily.

They passed through a small town, both of them looking longingly at the gas station, then continued on to Portland. Alex was on the verge of asking Thorn who they were going to see about gas money when he began talking about Natalie again.

It took every ounce of willpower Alex possessed not to ask him to stop. She hated hearing how beautiful Natalie was, how perfectly she walked, what her laughter sounded like. She was willing to give Natalie every benefit of every doubt but hearing Thorn wax poetically about her was getting tiresome.

He thinks of me as a friend, a buddy, a pal.

"It's her eyes," he mused.

"I know, I know, they're green like well water," Alex said, staring out her side of the car at a bucolic scene of pasture, cows and pond.

"What?"

Alex turned her attention back to him. He was staring at her. "What's wrong?"

He darted a quick glance at the mostly empty road ahead and then looked back at Alex. "I thought you were asleep last night."

Alex flinched. "Well, yes, that's true, I was asleep."

"What about the eyes as green as well water bit?"

She smiled sweetly. "I fell asleep right after that part."

"Why don't I believe you?"

Ignoring his question, she blurted out, "You know, Thorn, for an intelligent man, you're kind of dumb when it comes to women."

"Thanks a lot."

"For instance, why did you force Natalie into getting married so soon? If you'd waited a little longer, maybe this wouldn't have happened and—"

"Wait a second," he said, interrupting her. "Let's get one thing straight. Natalie is the one who wanted to get married right away. I was all for waiting."

So, Natalie had misled everyone at the shop. This information didn't come as a huge surprise, and in some ways, Alex even understood it. After all, no woman wants the whole town thinking *she's* the one doing the chasing, even if she is. Not that it sounded as though Thorn needed a whole lot of chasing to get caught. Apparently, a well-timed heaving of the bosom had been enough.

"I had misgivings, I admit that," he added.

"About marriage?"

"About Natalie. For instance, she didn't want to have children. Hell, my ranch is a family spread, passed down through three generations. From me it will go to my son—"

"Or daughter?"

"Daughter?"

"What if you don't have a boy?"

He furled his brow. "I never thought about that."

"But you just said Natalie didn't want to have children. That means no son—heck, for that matter, it means no daughter, either."

"I was sure she would change her mind."

Alex laughed.

He spared her a long, critical look. "What are you laughing about?"

"I've known Natalie Dupree for six months and I don't think I've ever seen her change her mind about anything."

"Until our wedding day," he said, staring straight ahead.

Oops! "Sorry. Anyway, with an issue as important as having a family or not at stake, I would have thought you'd insist on giving your relationship more time—"

"She threatened me," he interrupted.

Alex stared at his profile. "How?"

"She said she'd leave me."

Alex laughed again, she couldn't help herself.

This earned her an even stormier scowl from Thorn. "I'm glad my personal tragedy provides you with so much humor," he snarled.

"Tragedy? You're a lucky man, Thorn Powell. Don't you see that? You could have ended up with a woman who used sex—and don't bother denying it—to get you to the altar. Jeez, men."

"Now, wait a second—"

"No, I mean it. You're all a bunch of walking hormones without a logical bone in your muscular bodies."

Outside the car, the countryside whizzed by in a blur. Thorn, his chin determined, his eyes narrow, said, "This is priceless. Here you are, Miss Politically Correct, Miss Gender Sensitive, lumping all men into some hormone-crazed category because I happened to fall for a great-looking woman who could make—"

His words were cut off abruptly by a loud siren coming from the rear.

Thorn tore his attention from Alex and glanced in the

rearview mirror, then down at his speedometer. His fist crashed down hard on the top of the steering wheel as he swore. "Damn!"

Alex looked over her shoulder. "Oh, great," she said as she spied the police car, lights whirling, behind them. She'd been vaguely aware of their speed increasing as Thorn and she argued, but she'd been so caught up in his words that she hadn't stopped to think.

Thorn pulled the car over to the side of the road. He looked at Alex and sighed. She almost felt like laughing again.

They waited silently as the policeman got out of his car and approached them. He looked to be about thirty-five, a solid man with a dark mustache that didn't hide a frown. Thorn pushed down on the door handle.

"Just stay in the car, sir, please," the officer called.

Thorn stayed where he was.

The policeman glanced at Alex once, then twice, then turned his attention to Thorn. "My name is Officer Riggs. I clocked you on my radar going seventy-one miles an hour in a fifty-five-mile-an-hour zone. Would you have any legal reason to be speeding like that, sir?"

Thorn, sighing, said, "I wish I did."

"Will you take your license out of your wallet for me? I need your vehicle registration and your proof of insurance, as well."

Thorn turned to Alex. "The last two items are in a black folder in the glove box." He looked back at Riggs and added, "I'm afraid I don't have a driver's license in my possession, Officer. You see, I left in kind of a hurry. Well, actually it was my wedding day—"

"I see," Riggs commented as he produced a small notebook from his breast pocket. "Please give me your full name, sir, and your date of birth."

Thorn did so as Alex handed the proper papers to Officer Riggs. Riggs took all the information back to his car.

Looking over her shoulder, Alex saw Riggs reach inside the car and emerge with a hand-held radio. "What happens now?"

Thorn groaned. "I haven't the foggiest idea. This may come as a shock to you, but I've never been stopped for speeding before. And without a license? Probably a fine as big as this car."

"Thorn, I'm—"

"And did you see the way the man looked at you?"

"Looked at me?"

"Yes. You've got a black eye and a bandaged wrist, Alexandra. He probably thinks I'm a wife beater."

"I'm not your wife," she said as she looked at her face in the rearview mirror. Ooh, much more colorful than it had been a few hours before. A yellow semicircle cupped the bottom of her right eye, ringed with a blue line and a nice black smudge, punctuated with the scratches.

"I know you're not my wife," he said, staring back at the police car. "I've just gotten used to calling you that."

Officer Riggs put the radio back in his car, and again approached them. "Mr. Powell, are you aware, sir, that there is a warrant out for your arrest?"

Thorn's mouth literally fell open, then he snapped it shut with a roaring "What!"

"You have over six hundred dollars due in parking citations."

"I've never received a parking ticket in my entire life!" Thorn bellowed.

The officer looked at his notes. "They were all issued between February fifteenth and March first. Then there's failure to appear—"

"Wait a second, Officer. I wasn't even in Oregon the last two weeks of February." He turned to Alex. "There was a cattle breeders convention in Kansas City..." His voice trailed off, he swore and, shaking his head, his voice now heavy with suppressed anger, added, "Natalie. Her car was in the shop. I'd only known her for a few weeks, but she needed it and—"

"And her eyes turned your insides into mush," Alex said.

He cast her a quelling frown.

Officer Riggs cleared his throat. "I'm going to have to take you in."

"Wait a minute! I never even got a notice in the mail—"

"I'm afraid that's impossible, sir. Notices were sent."

"Maybe Natalie took them," Alex volunteered.

Thorn shook his head. "This can't be happening."

"Please step out of your car, sir. And you, ma'am, may I please see your license or some sort of identification?"

"I don't have any," she admitted.

Officer Riggs took her name and date of birth, walked back to his car, spoke on his radio and reappeared. During that time, Thorn stared morosely ahead. Alex wondered if he was more mortified by what was happening to him or by the thought that Natalie was in Seattle and, from the looks of things, they weren't going to be showing up at her hotel anytime in the near future.

"You check out fine, ma'am. Sir, is it okay with you if the lady drives your car back to the police station?"

Thorn's frown crumbled a bit as the absurdity of the situation apparently made its way past his pride. Chuckling deep in his chest, he cast Alex a sidelong look. "Is your wrist up to driving?"

"I'll be fine," she said.

"I imagine I'll get to make a free call. I could contact the ranch and have someone drive up here to bail me out, only…"

"Only what?" Alex prompted.

"Only I feel like a complete idiot," he admitted.

"And you don't want anyone at the ranch knowing about this?"

"Not on top of being stood up, I don't. I'll look like a world-class fool, but I can't see any other way—"

"Why don't you let me take care of it? I'll call my sister."

"I couldn't let you...."

"Sure you could. We're friends, remember?"

For a second he stared at her, and then slowly his lips formed a shy smile. "Thanks, Alexandra. I owe you one."

"You owe me about fifteen," she said.

He turned back to Riggs. "It's okay with me if she drives the car."

Thorn got out of the car, was handcuffed and shown to Riggs's back seat. The officer then returned to Alex, who had used the time to get behind the wheel.

"I have to ask you, Ms. Williams. Did Mr. Powell inflict your injuries—"

"Heavens no! I had an accident at the beach."

He nodded. She couldn't tell if he believed her or not. She smiled brilliantly and tried to look forthright, honest and sincere to belay his doubts. Thorn had enough problems without that one!

"Just follow me," Riggs said at last.

They drove back to the small town they'd traveled through a few minutes earlier. Alex parked in the space Officer Riggs pointed out. Riggs and Thorn disappeared around the back of the building. She went into the station.

Somewhere she'd read that pink was the color of choice for jails, that the color induced peaceful, calm feelings, a useful commodity in a police station. The walls in this place were painted the color of bile. If the color-affects-the-emotion-theory was correct, she couldn't begin to imagine what these walls did to people already stressed to the breaking point.

Scarred wooden benches ringed the waiting area. They were occupied by a handful of people who looked as though they'd been waiting since the day before the beginning of time. A few food and drink dispensers and two pay phones were at the back of the room while a counter ran along the front. The counter was joined to the ceiling by a wall of bars in which two windows had been cut. A half a dozen people worked behind the counter and didn't look up as Alex approached.

Eventually, a woman in her late fifties noticed Alex. She was wearing a tight green dress that, along with her body shape, made her look like an avocado. A kind face was crowned with graying curls. A pair of glasses rested on her chest, held there by a pearl chain.

Peering out through the bars with slightly myopic eyes, she clucked dismay. "Oh, my. Are you here to file an assault charge?"

Alex's good hand flew to touch her eye. "No, no, nothing like that. I'm here to find out what I can do to get Thorn Powell out of your jail."

"Oh, I see. That's the young man Officer Riggs is processing. Well, you just have a seat over there and I'll let you know when we get to that point."

Alex dutifully found an empty bench and sat. She was thirsty but reluctant to leave the waiting room to dig through the sack the Otter Point Inn had sent along for the lunch they'd never eaten. Since she didn't have a dime to her name, the soda machine wasn't any help, either. She spied a water fountain in a far corner and got a tepid drink from that, then she went into the bathroom to wash her hands. She wasn't sure why; she just felt as though she needed to wash her hands.

Thanks to the black eye that dominated her small face, the woman in the mirror was a ghastly sight. The rest of her was nothing to write home about, either, Alex thought as she took a look at her clothes. Even the silk flowers on her sandals looked wilted.

What in heck are you doing here? she asked her reflection. The answer lay deep in her heart, she knew that. It lay in the fog of Thorn's eyes, in the shape of his lips, in the vibrancy he faced life with and his vulnerable declaration that she was his friend.

"You're a world-class sucker. You know that, don't you?" she asked herself.

She went back to the waiting area and sat. A large clock visible through the bars showed the minutes pass, then the hours. Gradually the people in the waiting room were called to the counter and were sent away, but others replaced them. Alex had never been in a police station before. She realized her concept of it was colored by television sitcoms, and the real small-town station was decidedly more dull.

It was late afternoon before the woman with the gray curls finally called her name. "Miss Williams?"

Alex had been on the verge of nodding off when she heard her name. Jerking upright, she popped to her feet and briskly crossed the room. A glance at the clock showed that it was almost five. A hearty growl from her stomach reminded her the breakfast bagels had come and gone a long time ago.

"There now, I've got all the papers in order," the woman said.

Stifling a yawn, Alex was moved to ask, "What in the world took so long?"

She chuckled. "Well, now, it's funny, but there for a while, we lost Mr. Powell."

"You lost him! This is a police station. How can you lose someone?"

The woman put a finger over her lips. "Quiet, dear. It's really not as hard as it sounds. Officer Riggs put him in a locked room but then he was called away before he could tell anyone about it. No matter, we've found him now!"

Alex imagined she should be outraged, but she just couldn't quite work up the energy. "So now you're releasing him?"

"Oh, no, we couldn't do that. He either needs to post bond on his outstanding parking violations or appear two days from now when Judge Billings comes. Let's see... Speeding, parking violations, driving without a license in possession—"

Alex interrupted her. "How much money do we need to get him out of here?"

The woman consulted the top paper of a stack an inch thick. "Seven hundred fifty dollars."

"I'll get it. Where's your Western Union office?"

The woman giggled. "Oh, my dear, we don't have anything like that in this tiny little burg. You'll need to drive to Portland."

I don't have enough gas to drive to Portland! she screamed internally. She said, "Where's the closest bank?"

"You came in from the west entrance, right? Well, take the east door, cross the street and go two blocks. You can't miss it."

"Thanks."

"Of course, it closed a few minutes ago," the woman added as she glanced at the clock.

Alex shook her head. "Tell Mr. Powell that I'll get him out as soon as I can, that I haven't abandoned him."

The woman smiled broadly. "Forgive me for being so bold, dear, but I've seen the young man. Who would abandon *him?*"

"Natalie Dupree," Alex mumbled as she walked away from the counter.

She called the only person she could think of who would accept her collect call, do as asked and not suffer a heart attack in the process. She called her sister. Vicky's hello was nearly drowned out by a crying infant. "Alex, is that you?"

"It's me. Listen, don't ask any questions. I promise I'll explain later. I'm in Liberty, Oregon, and I need money.

There's a bank here and I'm pretty sure it's the same one you use.'' She mentioned the name.

"That's it. What do you need?"

"I need you to authorize the transfer of seven hundred fifty dollars first thing in the morning. No, wait. Make it for twenty dollars more because we desperately need gas. I don't have any identification, so you'll have to specify what I look like or give Mom's maiden name or something. I'll repay you the same day—"

"Are you in trouble—"

"No questions, Vic. I promise I'm okay."

"I'll call the bank first thing in the morning—"

"That's wonderful. Grab a pencil and write this down." Alex read the bank phone number out of the telephone book while the baby continued to cry in the background. "What's wrong with Emma?"

"Colic. Are you sure you're okay? Why aren't you at work—"

"It's a long story. By the way, you should be receiving an overnight delivery sometime tomorrow morning. I'll be there later in the day to pick it up. Me and a...friend, I mean. The delivery is for the friend."

"Okay."

"You're a doll," Alex said sincerely. "Suppose you can put us up for the night if we get a late start?"

Vicky's assurance and goodbye were swallowed by a newborn's cry.

Alex spent part of the evening in the convertible, first eating her share of the hotel food, then playing around with the buttons until she finally figured how to put the top up on the car so it could be locked securely. She considered sleeping in the car, but the parking lot was kind of dark and totally deserted, and she felt vulnerable and so alone. Finally she locked the rest of the food in the trunk and went back inside the police station.

New people, and fewer of them, were behind the counter. Alex got the attention of a young man with a prominent Adam's apple and asked if she could see Thorn for a few minutes. He told her he'd look into it. Within a half an hour, she was shepherded back to the men's detention area, which consisted of two cells. The first cell was occupied by a rumpled-looking man who had obviously had too much to drink. He looked at Alex with wild eyes and whistled.

"Knock it off, Eddie," the young officer snapped.

Thorn was in the second cell, seated on the lower of two bunks. He stood as Alex approached. She felt her heart thump painfully in her chest as she looked at him, and she wasn't sure if it was because he was locked up or because she wasn't locked up with him. He looked so forlorn....

"You have an admirer," he said, nodding in Eddie's direction.

Alex laughed. "I believe my current feminine charms are greatly enhanced by substance abuse. Listen, Thorn, I'm terribly sorry, but I won't have the money to get you out of here until tomorrow morning."

"I'm the one who's sorry," he said. "If I hadn't gotten angry and sped up, none of this would have happened."

"But I said things—"

"You said things that needed to be said." Running a hand through his hair, he added, "Who did you call about…this?"

"My sister. The money will be sent in the morning."

"Great."

Alex shook her head. "You know, you're a lot more calm than I thought you'd be."

He emitted a short bark of laughter, which was in no way mirthful. "Calm? Truth of the matter is I'm seething inside. You know what gets to me? I trusted her, that's what. She had to have gone through my mail and swiped those citations and she didn't even have the decency to pay them. This just makes one more thing Natalie is going to have to answer for."

It all circled back to Natalie. Always, back to Natalie. Well, what did you expect?

The officer cleared his throat. "Visiting hours are almost over."

"Just a minute more, please?" Alex begged.

He tapped his wristwatch.

Thorn said, "Right about now she's getting ready to dine with Mr. Ponytail. Damn, I hope they choke on their lobsters or that the pâté de foie gras gives them both a healthy dose of food poisoning." He looked alarmed, and added, "Hell, I didn't think about this before, but what if they check out of the Red Swan—"

"Don't do this to yourself. Just get through the night, and tomorrow we'll start again."

He stared at Alex for several seconds before mumbling, "You're right."

Seeking to leave him with a smile, she added, "In a lighter vein, I heard they lost you today."

"Lost me?"

"Didn't you know?"

"I know I sat in a room for an eternity before they finally put me in here."

"That's when they lost you." She touched a bar with one finger and added, "Just be sure they don't lose you again."

Her words somehow hovered in the air between them, almost intimate, much more meaningful than a strict interpretation could justify. Alex felt it and she suspected Thorn did, too, because his eyebrows raised ever so slightly. He came a step closer. He reached forward, but a stern shake of the head from the young officer stilled this movement. "What are you going to do tonight? Where are you going to sleep?"

"Don't worry about me," she told him. "You just worry about yourself."

"What's to worry about? Here I am in the Taj Mahal. I've got hot food, a warm bed and the jolly whistler down there to keep me company. But what about you, Alexandra?" He looked at the officer. "Listen, she's here all alone with no money and no bed for the night—"

"Stop, Thorn," Alex said, embarrassed at being described to the officer as some homeless waif. She looked right into Thorn's eyes and added, "You promised to stay out of my personal life, remember? Just let me take care of myself."

The officer touched her arm. "It's time, miss."

Alex nodded. It seemed so odd to see Thorn behind bars. She had the overwhelming desire to hold him. The memory of his body next to hers the night before suddenly rushed through her mind—his heat, his breathing, his voice, soft and drowsy.

They'd been apart six hours, and it seemed like six weeks.

Thorn grinned at her. "Keep your chin up," he said.

She was so overcome with intense feelings for him that she was temporarily speechless. With a final smile, she left the area quickly, two steps ahead of the officer.

Chapter Six

Alex's hope was that the last few nights of interrupted sleep would somehow soften the wooden bench on which she sat, with her head back against the wall, her eyes closed. No such luck. Police stations didn't dim the lights, didn't dispense pillows and blankets, didn't turn down the volume on the human problems that marched through the door day and night.

When morning finally rolled around, she found herself more tired than she had been when the night began. There was a sandbox behind her eyes; her limbs were heavy and uncoordinated. She used the bathroom to wash out her mouth and splash her face, to untangle her hair and force it into submission with an unattended rubber band she'd swiped off the counter, to shake out her sweatshirt and reluctantly pull it back on over her head.

By the time these modified morning absolutions were taken care of, it was almost time for the bank to open. Alex used the east door as directed and walked along unfamiliar streets, relieved beyond words when she found a woman in the process of unlocking the bank door.

As Alex explained to first one official and then another what she wanted, she was met with incredulous stares. At last, one stern-looking man set her straight. "Listen, Miss Williams. Yes, we got a call from your sister, and yes, she authorized us to give you money, but it's absolutely out of the question. I'll tell you what I told her—you can't transfer money across state lines like that. And frankly, even if it was possible, I wouldn't do it. You don't have a shred of identification and you don't have an account with us. There's absolutely nothing we can do to help."

Alex finally admitted defeat. There was no way around it; she was simply going to have to tell Thorn to call his ranch. She was disappointed not to be able to help him, but there just weren't any other options.

The woman with the curls was back at work. Officer Riggs was standing at her desk and both of them were staring at a computer screen.

Alex cleared her throat. Riggs nodded politely while the woman came to the counter.

Alex explained the situation, ending with, "So, please, either let me talk to Thorn or tell him yourself. He'll have to call the ranch, he'll have to get someone to bring the money."

Riggs stepped over to the counter. He bit his lip, looked at the clock, stared relentlessly at Alex and drummed his fingers against the counter. At last, he said, "Grace, issue Thorn Powell a citation to appear in thirty days. Let's get these people out of here."

Alex felt weak in the knees as she gripped the counter. The fleeting wish that this conclusion had been reached the day before was just that: fleeting. "Officer Riggs, I think I love you!"

Riggs cracked his first smile.

Like magic, Thorn was released from his cell and given both the citation and strict orders to return home at once and reclaim his driver's license.

As Alex patted her pockets for the keys, Thorn pushed through the doors and broke out into the sunlight.

"Boy, am I glad that's over," he said with gusto. He looked down at Alex, grinned and suddenly swooped her into his arms, making a half turn as he did so. Alex flung her arms around his neck to steady herself, and laughed with him, her sprained wrist all but forgotten. At last he took a deep breath, and looking into Alex's eyes, added, "I'm a free man again and it feels great!"

"A free man with a criminal record," she teased. She spoke with great difficulty. His face was so close. His lips were beautiful, full and succulent. She wanted to breach the four inches that separated them and taste his mouth. Instead, she said, "Did you get any sleep? Did the whistler bother you much?"

"Ah, good old Eddie. Not only did he whistle, but he also held lengthy conversations with himself. The only sleep I got was after they finally released him this morning. Where's the car, Alexandra?"

She was mesmerized by the look of his throat as he spoke, by the movement of his chin and jaw. He needed a shave. In fact, he looked almost as crumpled as she did and it endeared him to her in an unexpected way.

"Alexandra?"

She finally tore her gaze away from Thorn and looked toward the parking space. "Right there—"

The words died on her lips. The car was gone.

He put her down. "Did you move it?"

"No," she said, still disbelieving her eyes. The car had to be there. It wasn't, though, and as her gaze swept the parking lot, which was way too small to conceal Thorn's car, she felt sick to her stomach.

"Blast it all to hell!" Thorn roared.

"Maybe the police moved it," she suggested as she dug in her pockets for the keys and came up empty.

"Why would *they* move *my* car?"

"I don't know, but it's the only logical answer—"

"No, Alexandra, I'm afraid it's not the only logical answer. Maybe someone stole it! Damn, damn, damn, damn!" he chanted as he paced around the empty spot as though he could make the car reappear. "Some jerk has driven off in my car. It's probably stripped by now. Damn!"

"We have to check inside, Thorn. Perhaps Riggs moved it—"

"Oh, believe me, I know we have to check inside. For one thing, you watch, I'm going to have to file a stolen vehicle form and then I need to call my insurance company—damn!"

Alex took a deep breath and followed in his wake. Officer Riggs was still at Grace's desk. They both looked up as Thorn and Alex approached the counter.

"My car is gone," Thorn stated flatly.

Riggs took a few steps toward them. "What do you mean, gone?"

"Gone. Vanished. Stolen."

Riggs looked confused. "It was there a couple of hours ago when I came on duty."

"Well, it's not there now."

Alex groaned. "Then you didn't move it?"

Riggs's eyebrows rose. "Why would *I* move it? I don't even have the keys."

The woman tapped a pencil against Riggs's arm. She said, "Eddie. We released Eddie an hour ago."

Riggs shook his head. "That damn Eddie. He's the only one stupid enough to steal a car out of a police station parking lot in broad daylight. Wait a second—since when does Eddie know how to hot-wire a car?"

The sick feeling in Alex's stomach stampeded up her throat as she croaked out, "He might not need to know how. I think I may have left the keys in the trunk lock. I remember putting the rest of the food in the trunk last night, but I don't remember having the keys after that, and I can't find them now.''

Three people stared at her as though she was the dumbest creature on the face of the earth. Alex smiled weakly, contritely. Finally Riggs snapped into action. ''Grace, I saw Mr. Powell's vehicle registration yesterday, so go ahead and get started on an unauthorized use of a motor vehicle. I'll get on the radio.''

''You left the keys to a forty-five-thousand-dollar car in the lock?'' Thorn squeaked.

''I think so.'' Alex wished she could fade away. ''I'm awfully sorry—''

''So am I,'' Thorn said as he accepted the papers Grace handed him. He looked back at Riggs and added, ''And you might start looking for my car at the closest gas station.''

Alex found herself back on the wooden bench, staring at the putrid yellow walls, which, come to think of it, adequately reflected the way she felt. By now, she knew every crack in the plaster, every depressing notice pinned to the bulletin board. Even the people who sat near her looked familiar, as though their day job was to sit on a bench at the police station and...wait. She would have killed for a shower and a change of clothes, to say nothing of a couple of aspirin to ease the pain in her wrist.

Thorn was on the verge of placing a collect call to his insurance company when Riggs burst back into the room. ''We found it!'' he yelled.

The phone was slammed back into place as both Thorn and Alex rushed to the counter.

Riggs, the flush of success on his face, elaborated. ''It was old Eddie, all right. He apparently made a quick stop at the store, bought himself a six-pack of beer, drove out Highway 99, ran out of gas and fell asleep. Stevens says he's still there. We'll arrange to have the car towed—''

Thorn shook his head. "If you tow it and impound it, we're stuck here. You know the story, you know I don't have my wallet. No money, no credit cards—"

"Yeah, and Natalie to find," Riggs added.

Alex, stunned, stared at Thorn.

"Well, we talked in the patrol car on the way into the station yesterday," he explained.

"Come with me," Riggs said with authority. "I'll give you a ride to the car, we won't tow it. You filled out the papers, right? Good, no reason to keep you guys here."

They rode in the back of the patrol car, sitting side by side. Alex stared out the window and prayed that they would find Thorn's car in one piece and with no major parts missing. Meanwhile, Thorn and Riggs talked about the newest basketball player to join the Trailblazers. Men were truly amazing creatures.

They found another patrol car parked beside the convertible. Eddie, seated in the back, waved merrily as they walked past his door.

Officer Stevens was younger than Riggs, a big blond man with freckles and an infectious grin. He carried a torn paper bag, through which peeked several open cans of beer. He handed Riggs the car keys and said, "Eddie told me he found them in the trunk lock and just decided on the spur of the moment to take himself on a little ride. Silly old fool." He smiled politely at Thorn and Alex before returning to his car where he made a U-turn and started back toward town.

Riggs handed the keys to Thorn. "I've got a gasoline can in my trunk for emergencies," he said.

As the two men emptied the gas into the car, Alex sat in the passenger seat and rewrapped her wrist with the bandage. The top was down again and the smell of beer was slowly but surely dissipating.

"Take this," Riggs said as Thorn got in behind the wheel.

Alex saw a twenty-dollar bill in the officer's outstretched hand.

Thorn protested.

"Just take it," Riggs insisted. "Buy yourself some gas at the first station you get to, go get your wallet and send me twenty bucks."

"But—"

"Take it," Riggs repeated, and thrust it into Thorn's hand.

Thorn, relenting, took the money. "I'll send it to you—"

"I know you will. Now get out of here." His gaze rested on Alex briefly and he added, "And, ma'am, next time, watch where you leave the keys."

"I plan to," Alex said.

"There won't be a next time," Thorn rumbled, ruining the effect only slightly with a reluctant smile.

Riggs slapped the driver's door a couple of times. Thorn nodded his thanks in a manly fashion, which seemed to obliterate the need for spoken words, then started the engine. He, too, made a U-turn, and once again, they were on their way.

Alex fell asleep before the gas station disappeared in the rearview mirror.

There was a pool of water, deep and cool, and she was naked, swimming freely. She was a fish, then a mermaid and then just herself. Wait. Someone else was in the pool. Thorn reached out both his hands and cupped her face. As they spun toward the bottom, legs entwined, he lowered his mouth to hers. His lips tasted like ripe fruit, and as he held her close, she shivered.

And then the water was green, green. It was a well she was suspended in and Thorn was gone. Well water, green like well water...

"Alexandra?"

Alex's eyes fluttered open. Thorn was staring at her.

She swallowed and blinked a few times. "Where are we?" she asked. Her voice sounded hoarse.

"Almost in Tacoma, at a truck stop. I don't know how to get to your sister's house."

Alex nodded as she sat up straight. Her cheek felt damp. Good grief, had she been drooling?

"Do I go all the way into town?"

She rubbed her sleeve against her cheek. "Ah, no. Give me a second to wake up here and I'll tell you how to get there."

He waited patiently for Alex to recover from sleep. What she was really doing was recovering from her dream. It had seemed so real. She could still recall the taste of his mouth and the strength of his arms and the feel of his bare skin pressed against her before the dream had changed, before he'd been replaced by Natalie's eyes.

"Alexandra, I have a favor to ask of you," he said.

She looked up at him. "Sure."

He bit his lip, then stared at his hands, which were hooked over the steering wheel. "I don't expect you to lie to your sister about why we needed money sent to us, but you have to admit, it's really embarrassing."

"Oh, but you shouldn't be embarrassed. She's my sister."

"Your sister, not mine. Anyway, I was just hoping that you hadn't mentioned my being stood up at the altar to her."

Alex was surprised by this but she said truthfully, "I didn't. She doesn't know a thing about it."

"Then I would appreciate it if we kept it that way. I just feel like such a fool—"

"No problem," Alex said quickly.

He nodded curtly. "Good. Thanks. Now, how do we get there?"

Alex's directions were only slightly confused; it had been two years since she'd visited Vicky's home and a few wrong turns were inevitable, but eventually, they rolled up in front of the house. Thanks to the car being stolen, it was late afternoon by this time, but the sun was still warm and the suburban street mostly deserted.

"That's odd," Alex said as she got out of the car.

He closed his door, stretched and said, "What's odd?"

"The sprinkler is on but it's aimed at one side of Vicky's car, not the grass."

As they approached the car, they realized that its engine was running and the windshield wipers were going back and forth, back and forth. Just visible inside the car was Alex's sister.

Alex braved the sprinkler and tapped on the glass. She saw Vicky's head jerk around and a smile pull her lips apart.

The door opened and Vicky emerged, darting past Alex to avoid the sprinkler. She was an inch taller than Alex and had cut her auburn hair since Alex last saw her. Wearing white cotton slacks and a light blue T-shirt, she was also fuller in the bust, thanks, no doubt, to the fact that she was breast-feeding her new daughter.

"You look great," Alex said as they hugged.

Vicky held Alex at arm's length. Alex could tell she'd been about ready to return the compliment, but the words died on her lips.

"Good grief, Alex! What in the world has happened to you?"

"I crashed into a beach," Alex said, wincing as Vicky grabbed her hands. "My wrist, my wrist!"

Vicky dropped Alex's hand. "Are you okay? I've been so worried. The bank laughed at me when I told them what you wanted to do. Jeff and I were going to drive down there tonight if you hadn't shown up—"

"I'll explain it all after a long shower," Alex promised.

As Vicky's gaze drifted over Alex's shoulder, she seemed aware for the first time that they weren't alone.

Speculation sparked Vicky's eyes as she stared at Thorn. Alex could see it. She suddenly wished they'd had the wallet sent to the Red Swan Hotel in Seattle. She'd forgotten what a matchmaker Vicky was.

Alex sighed inwardly and introduced Thorn. A smile reserved for attractive men who might be interested in her little sister curved Vicky's lips as she stepped past Alex and took Thorn's hand. "It must be your package that came in the mail today," she said. "It's in the house."

Thorn looked weak with relief. "Thanks—"

"Oh, it's no bother. Anything for one of Alex's *friends*."

Alex, hoping to divert the direction this conversation was headed, said, "What were you doing in the car with the sprinkler on and the windshield wipers—"

"Oh my gosh, the baby!" Vicky interrupted. She dashed around the car to open the drier passenger door, and Alex was suddenly aware of a baby's cries. A few minutes later, after the car was turned off, Vicky emerged with a blanket, and tucked inside lay Alex's niece.

A tiny scrunched-up face the color of a strawberry greeted Alex's eyes as she peered at the baby.

"Do you want to hold her?" Vicky asked hopefully.

Alex took the baby, who continued to cry, her small hands balled up into fists.

"Colic," Vicky said succinctly. She smiled at Thorn and then added, "She does this a lot. Cry, I mean. A whole lot."

Thorn said, "She's adorable."

Vicky nodded. Alex had the idea that Vicky couldn't quite see "adorable" right this minute.

He was right though, Emma was a cutie. Bald and red, but with definite potential. Alex hadn't spent much time with infants and she studied her niece's face with interest. Maybe Mom's nose, definitely Jeff's eyes. She imagined the little mouth was sweet when it was actually closed. This was her niece, bound to her with blood ties, and for a second, Alex felt the primal urge to have a baby of her own, to mother a child.

"I'm so glad you're spending the night," Vicky said over her shoulder as she led the way to the front door. "It will be so nice to catch up. I've already started a roast and Jeff is going to try to get off a little early." She stopped talking over her daughter's cries and turned to Alex. "Here, give Emma to me. I'll go change a diaper or something. Get your luggage and take the room over the garage. It's the only quiet room we currently have. You'll have to use the downstairs bath."

As soon as Vicky disappeared inside the house, Thorn caught Alex's arm. "We're spending the night?" he whispered.

"I mentioned it to her over the phone. I guess she didn't understand that it wasn't for sure. Listen, Thorn, you go on if you want, but I'm too tired for words." Truth of the matter was that he looked even more tired than she did.

"I can't run out without at least eating dinner," he said.

Alex smiled. She was inordinately glad he was staying, at least for a while. "And maybe a shower and a change of clothes?" she added.

He seemed to think for a second, an act that ended in a deep yawn. "Hell, I can't face Natalie like this. I'm going to have to chance that she'll stay at the Red Swan for another day, and get a decent night's sleep. But what about this single room over the garage?"

"Vicky obviously thinks you and I are lovers. If you don't want me telling her the truth of the matter, I'm going to have to think of something else—"

"Couldn't we just camp out together?" he asked hopefully. "I mean, it's not as though it would be the first night we've spent in the same room, and I hate to put you in the position of lying to your sister."

"Well, she did say it was the only quiet room in the house—"

"That's right."

Alex thought of their options. "What the heck," she said at last and was rewarded with a grateful smile.

He stared at the sprinkler, which was still hitting Vicky's car. "Why was she sitting in the car with the water—?"

"I haven't the foggiest idea," Alex said, "but while you get your suitcase out of the trunk, I'll turn off the sprinkler."

Thorn opened his wallet and greeted the credit cards, paper bills and photographs folded within like they were long-lost friends. Wait, photographs! He dug through a stack of them until he found the one he'd been searching for.

Natalie on a horse, hair disheveled beautifully, eyes blazing. He'd insisted she take a ride on Sprite, his gorgeous white Arabian mare, and she'd finally agreed. When he'd snapped the photo, he'd thought she looked excited. Now he saw that she was angry, spitting nails kind of angry. Thorn tore the picture into tiny little pieces of confetti and sprinkled them into the garbage can.

He'd borrowed an envelope from Vicky and immediately stuck twenty dollars inside along with a short note of thanks, then addressed it to Riggs, care of the Liberty, Oregon, Police Station.

That done, he spied his phone calling card and used it to call Information. Upon receiving the phone number, he placed a call to the Red Swan Hotel, where he asked if Gerald and Jasmine Blackwell were registered. The female operator answered in the affirmative.

Off the top of his head, he concocted a story about being Gerald's brother. "I missed a plane connection," he said, trying to sound properly distressed. "His birthday party is tonight and now I'm going to miss it."

The operator sounded young and sympathetic. "Don't

you just hate it when the airlines don't keep their schedules? What a shame about your brother and all.''

"I know, I'm just sick about it."

"I'll put your call through to his room—"

"No, no, don't do that. It was a...a surprise party but now the surprise is I'll be a day late. I guess what I need to know is, will Gerald and Jasmine still be there?"

"Let me check the reservation card," the helpful operator said. She came back on the line after only a few seconds. "Oh, you're in luck! Your brother will be with us for two more days."

Bingo! "Thanks," he told her. "You've been a huge help. And remember, don't tell him I called." He set the phone down on the floor and sighed deeply. There was nothing more he could do now, and the thought of inaction, which he would have expected to fill him with angst, didn't faze him.

"I'm just too damn tired to care," he mumbled to himself as he sat back in the chair. The room to which he and Alexandra had retreated was indeed over the garage. The bed was pushed up against the southern wall, flanked on one side by an old oak hope chest and on the other with a beat-up dresser. The only other furniture in the room was the big upholstered chair in which he currently sat.

He wondered if he'd be spending the night in the chair. All Alexandra had said was, "I get the first shower," before skipping back down the stairs into the house.

The faint sound of a baby crying filtered up the interior stairwell. Thorn stood and walked to the window where he could look down at his car. He had been so relieved when they'd recovered it that morning. He was fond of the big old thing. He smiled to himself as he recalled the look of horror that had flared in Alexandra's eyes when she admitted leaving the keys in the lock. He knew a few men who couldn't tell the difference between a woman and a car, but he'd always prided himself in not being so wrapped up in mechanical things that he lost sight of what they really were. Still—

He heard feet on the stairs and turned as Alexandra walked through the door. If it wasn't for the black eye, he didn't know if he would have recognized her. Her hair was dry and curly, framing her face, which was barely touched by makeup. She was wearing a sleeveless white blouse tucked into denim shorts. A narrow brown belt emphasized her slender waist and matched the leather sandals she wore on her feet.

"You look terrific," he said. And she did. For the first time, he was aware of her as a woman and not just as a steadfast pal. That wasn't strictly true, he admitted, as he recalled the sight of her in the blue bathing suit, the sight of her wrapped up in a robe, the heft and warmth of her body he'd noticed when he'd picked her up and spun her around.

Tilting his head, he watched her walk around the room, examining the knickknacks on a shelf, smoothing the worn pink chenille spread on the bed. She was like a stranger. It suddenly seemed all wrong to spend the night with her, and yet at the same time, entirely right.

Wild thoughts!

"You'd better go take a shower," she told him. "Dinner is almost ready and Jeff will be home momentarily. And don't worry, I know how tired you are. I've explained almost everything to Vicky and she's promised not to be offended if you wander off right after dinner and put a lid on this day."

"You didn't mention Natalie—"

"No. Vicky thinks you and I are dating. I'll just let her believe it. Next month, I'll tell her you're an unmitigated heel and that I broke up with you!"

"Oh, great—"

"Get going," she said, smiling.

* * *

He took a long shower and scraped the beard off his face. He put on fresh clothes—tan shorts and a creamy linen shirt with the tiniest of beige stripes running through the fabric. Vacation clothes. Honeymoon clothes. He yearned for his jeans and his boots.

For a few seconds, he leaned against the sink. His eyes were dark and forbidding as he stared into the mirror. It was Tuesday, three short days since his aborted wedding. Natalie seemed more and more like a figment of his imagination, and yet the desire to confront her burned just as brightly in his heart as it had the moment he'd opened her closet and come face-to-face with her discarded wedding gown.

How dare she put him through this! If she thought for one second that he was going to crawl back to the ranch and let her off the hook, then she was sorely mistaken. He'd find her all right, and when he did, he'd humiliate her in front of Gerald Blackwell the same way she'd humiliated him in front of his family and his friends and all the people he worked with day after day. Only then would he stop and go back home. Revenge was sweet, they said, and he was anxious for a big juicy bite of it.

Revenge? Was this what his determination to find Natalie had turned into? Revenge? What about loose ends and all that? "Nothing wrong with a little revenge," he said, grinning.

Vicky wasn't really much of a cook—the roast was dry, the vegetables overcooked, the pie too sweet—but she was a nice woman and her husband, Jeff, seemed a reasonable fellow. They talked sports and babies—*Did Thorn want a family someday?*—and then Vicky began touting Alexandra's virtues. Thorn smiled secretly, wondering if there was ever a time in his life when he wouldn't have seen through Vicky's motives. He guessed that there probably had been and maybe even that it hadn't been that long ago. After all, Natalie had hoodwinked him.

Besides, it wasn't fair to judge Vicky. They were sitting in her living room under false pretenses; she had no way of knowing there was no romance going on.

"So, Thorn," Vicky said, "Alex says you're a rancher." He nodded. "That's right."

She smiled. "Is there any money in ranching?"

"Vicky!" This, from Alexandra.

"There's enough money to keep me comfortable," he said evasively.

"Alexandra has a way with animals. Doesn't she, Jeff?"

Thorn was amused to see Jeff struggle to find the right words for something he apparently wasn't sure about. "Uh, yes," he finally said.

Vicky, undeterred, added, "By the time she got into high school, she'd managed to bring home five cats. Remember, Alex?"

Thorn snuck a peek at Alexandra as she mumbled her answer. She was shooting decidedly pointed looks at Vicky, who was ignoring her. He decided to help out; after all, what were friends for?

"What was the deal with the car and the sprinkler?" he asked right after Vicky recounted Alexandra's high school scholastic record.

Jeff looked perplexed. "What car and sprinkler?"

Vicky slid a shy smile toward her husband. "I've discovered that if I turn the engine and the wipers on and then get water to hit the car like it's raining, Emma will actually go to sleep. I figure it takes less gas to do that than to actually drive around, and I get the advantage of a little nap for myself. I'm very careful to close the windows on the sprinkler side but I leave the other side open because the engine is running."

"I don't think this is a good idea," Jeff said sternly. "Besides, honey, isn't it rather excessive?"

Vicky smiled sweetly, a smile Thorn had seen on Alexandra's face, a smile that answered what she thought was a silly question without a single word being uttered. *Good grief! He was beginning to recognize Alexandra's expressions even when they were on someone else's face!* He looked at Alexandra, but her eyes were downcast and she was holding her wrist as though it hurt.

Jeff shook his head. "Anyway, how about a game of cards, or maybe we could rent a movie?"

"Not for me," Thorn said. "I'm sorry, but I'm dead on my feet."

Vicky stood. "Don't worry about it. Jeff still thinks like a man without a baby in the house."

Jeff looked at his wife. "And what does that mean?"

"It means your daughter has been asleep for two hours. She's been fussing for the past fifteen minutes, which means she'll be screaming any second."

"I haven't heard her fussing."

"Trust me on this," Vicky said dryly.

Jeff looked at Thorn. "Emma has colic."

"Yes, I know."

Right on cue, a cry came from down the hall. Vicky smiled smugly as she turned to her sister. "You and Thorn go on up to bed." The way she said it was loaded, loaded, loaded. It actually caused Alexandra's cheeks to color.

As Vicky stood, she added, "Be sure to close the door at the top of the stairs and put pillows over your heads."

Thorn took Alex's good hand in his, meeting her startled eyes with a grin. "Coming, sweetheart?" This was kind of fun....

"Of course, darling," she told him, grinning right back.

He was also beginning to notice that she adjusted to situations with the speed of a lightning bolt. Hmm—

"Take these," he said later, holding out a glass of water and two aspirin.

Alex was in the bed. He'd caught a glimpse of a pink nightgown, short and sassy, before she'd pulled the covers up over her chest. Now all that showed were two little pink straps, one of which had slipped down her arm.

As she took the pills and downed them with the water, he tore his eyes away from that errant strap and chided himself. Where were all these thoughts about Alexandra coming from? *Natalie. Concentrate on Natalie.*

He gestured toward the chair. "Do you want me to sleep on that?"

Yawning again, she said, "No. Don't be silly. Just get into bed."

"Do I get to get under the covers?" he asked, smiling down at her.

She returned his smile. "No. There's an extra blanket in the dresser drawer. You can sleep on the bedspread."

"How do you know there's a blanket in the drawer?"

"I've stayed here before, of course."

Thorn opened the drawer. "No blanket."

"Check the other drawer."

He did as requested, coming up empty-handed. "I'll go track down your sister and ask her for a blanket," he said. "She shouldn't be hard to find. I'll just follow the crying baby—"

"Just get in the bed," Alex interrupted, "and stay on your own side."

He was wearing his silk boxer shorts again, and he noticed that she looked away with an alarmed expression flashing across her pretty features as he pulled off the T-shirt and slipped under the sheets. Maybe he should have kept the T-shirt on; maybe it would have made her more comfortable. But as he usually slept in the buff, the shorts alone were a concession. Too late now; he couldn't very well get out of bed and start putting clothes *on*.

Besides, there was a line down the middle of the bed as inviolate as a barbed-wire fence. He could feel it and he knew she could, too. He wondered for a while if he should talk to her, tell her how nice her family was, maybe tease her about her sister's obvious ploys to make her look good, or chastise her for listening to him blab on and on about Natalie two nights before without revealing she was awake. While he thought of a good opening gambit, the last few days caught up with him and he fell asleep.

Alex lay awake, every nerve end tingling. *He was so close!* Because of the streetlight coming in the window opposite the bed she could see his profile. His eyes were closed and his breathing was so even and steady that he had to be asleep.

She thought about the look of him as he got into bed, the way the silk moved across his rear when he stretched, the breadth of his shoulders, the glow of his bare skin. So close…

And yet so far away. So very far away.

Damn Vicky! Alex had asked her for a nightgown and Vicky had handed over this little pink number, swearing it was *the* only clean nightie she owned. Now the thin layer of satin did little to shield her body against the growing warmth of Thorn's body. She carefully reached beneath the covers and tugged on the nightgown, smoothing it down her legs as far it would stretch, which wasn't far.

Alex closed her eyes but her mind was a whirlwind of thoughts. She was growing impatient with Thorn, which wasn't very nice, but it hurt to help him move heaven and earth to find a woman who wasn't half-good enough for him. And yet she felt compelled to try. In her heart of hearts she couldn't help but wonder if a man who didn't love a woman would take so much time and energy to track her down just to confront her.

She was tired enough that it hurt to think and yet contrarily, it seemed that was all she could do. Tomorrow they would catch up with Natalie. Tomorrow, Thorn would confront her, say all the things that were eating away at him inside, and then they would go back to Cottage Grove. Would she ever see him again? It was hardly likely he'd come into the flower shop—too many painful memories.

She admitted to herself that she'd succumbed to morbid curiosity. She *was* looking forward to seeing Natalie's face when her actions caught up with her. Natalie hadn't actually done a thing to Alex personally—with the possible exception of the awful dress currently residing in Thorn's trunk—but as Alex's feelings for Thorn expanded, so did her anger with Natalie.

Tomorrow would bring a conclusion to this adventure, a resolution to Thorn's wounded feelings and pride, and after what she'd been through with him, the payoff would be witnessing it.

Was this as sick as it sounded? She couldn't tell. It sounded reasonable, and that in itself was kind of alarming!

A soft mumble came from Thorn's lips. He thrashed out once at the sheets, and muttered something else, obviously in the throes of a dream.

Instinctively, Alex reached out to comfort him.

She was startled when he grabbed her arms with forceful hands and pulled her to his chest, crushing her against him, his embrace burning and powerful.

She tried rousing him. "Thorn?"

One of his hands moved up behind her neck and pulled her face forward until her lips were pressed against his. As she struggled to free herself, his grip lessened and she was free to move away as far as she wished, but the character of the kiss changed in that instant, became less aggressive and more passionate, and she found she didn't want to move. Instead, she succumbed to his lips, succumbed to his caress. There was nothing but him, his mouth, his hands, his body.

She'd wanted this encounter for days; she realized this now. As his hand ran down her side, she groaned with anticipation. She made her mind stop questioning the wisdom of this kiss and what was to follow. Just him, his mouth, warm and moist, his hands, tender but insistent, knowing.

Slowly she realized his demands had lessened, that he'd drifted away from her without actually moving. His hand slid from her hip. She was half-pinned under his arm, his chin next to her mouth.

"Thorn?" she whispered.

No answer. Just steady breathing and the weight of his arm. He was asleep!

Good heavens, how could he go to sleep in the middle of something like this!

Wait, wait, who had the man kissed: Alexandra Williams or Natalie Dupree?

It hadn't been a first kiss, gentle and exploring. It had been the kiss of a man who knew the woman he was kissing intimately, who knew exactly what she wanted and how to give it to her.

"You're a damn fool," she mumbled, not sure as to which one of them she referred, yet knowing that ultimately, the label fit them both.

Chapter Seven

The next morning, they discovered the hard way that Vicky's vague directions for reaching the interstate were lacking in some serious details. Ultimately they wound up in the hills above Puget Sound near a construction site. As Thorn worked at turning the car around in a driveway that was more dirt than concrete, Alex looked out at the deep blue water, dotted here and there with white sails.

She sighed with pleasure. "Isn't it beautiful?"

"Isn't what beautiful?" He was turning the car back onto the rutted road.

"The water and the boats. Do you like to go sailing, Thorn?"

He braked the car and stared over her shoulder at the water. "It's okay. I've only been out a few times on a friend's boat down in Newport. How about you?"

"Never been, but I think it looks so relaxing."

"I prefer to relax in my pickup or on the back of my horse," he said.

"I love to ride horses."

He stared at her for a second. "I didn't know you rode."

"You don't know much about me at all," she said gently.

"That's not true. Thanks to your sister, I know quite a lot about you."

"Oh, that—"

"She was about as subtle as a raging river, but it was kind of cute. Anyway, when did you learn how to ride a horse?"

"As a child. Our neighbors had a little pinto, which they sometimes let me and Vicky ride around their pasture. I loved it."

"My favorite horse right now is a white mare. An Arabian. Truth of the matter is that I'm really too big for her. She's kind of a delicate little thing. Natalie rode her once or twice."

Alex stared into his eyes and said, "I have a hard time imagining Natalie on a horse."

"Well, you're right. It wasn't until about twelve hours ago that I realized how actively she disliked it. I'd show you a picture of Sprite—that's my horse—but I tore it into little pieces last night. Natalie was in the picture, too."

Alex nodded silently. Hovering in her mind was the impact that his nocturnal kiss had had on her, and yet he hadn't mentioned a thing about it. Now he was saying Natalie's name, bitterness tainting his voice. Though it was better than wistful regret, it was obvious she was still front and center in his mind. And yet, the kiss, the kiss. She'd lain awake half the night reviewing it. It had started as one thing and ended as another, but did *that* matter?

This was confusing! She said, "You know, we got kind of a late start this morning and now, thanks to Vicky, who knows where we're at?"

"I do," he said with assurance. Moving the car along the road, he added, "Speaking of a late start, what did you and Vicky talk about all morning?"

Alex shrugged. "Sister stuff." She chuckled when she

thought of Vicky's parting advice, given in a whisper. "Hold on to this one," she'd said. "That guy is gorgeous and he's crazy about you." It had been on the tip of Alex's tongue to say, *No, he's not crazy about me, he's just crazy, period.*

"What are you laughing about?" Thorn asked.

"My sister. She's such a little matchmaker."

"I noticed." He glanced quickly at her and added, "I liked her, though."

"Well, trust me. She liked you, too."

"Good."

"I mean, really liked you. In her mind, we're engaged and about to tie the knot." Alex giggled and added, "Imagine that!"

Thorn looked at her as he regained a paved road, a sign pointing the right way to get to the interstate. "I don't know if I appreciate the note of derision I hear in your voice," he said.

"What do you mean?"

"I mean that you sound incredulous that Vicky could imagine you marrying me. What's wrong with me?"

"Nothing is wrong with you," she said quickly.

"Then why wouldn't you marry me?"

She stared at him with shocked eyes until it finally hit her that she'd unknowingly stumbled onto a jilted man's most easily bruised body part—his ego. He didn't mean the question as it sounded, he didn't mean that he could imagine marrying *her,* Alexandra Williams, so why couldn't *she* imagine marrying *him?* There was nothing whatsoever personal about his question!

It infuriated her! She wasn't sure exactly why except that he wasn't the only one in the car with an ego that was being batted around like a softball at a company picnic.

"Answer me," he demanded as they finally merged onto the freeway.

"Because you're...well, Thorn, truth of the matter is that you're—"

"Go on," he said, darting a glance at her.

She plucked a word from her youth. "You're shallow!"

"I'm shallow?"

"Yes, I'm afraid you are."

"You'd better explain yourself," he said, his voice now angry.

"Natalie this and Natalie that, but always the way she looked or laughed or moved, never how she felt or what she said or what she dreamed about."

"Now wait a second, that's not true."

"Isn't it? Think."

He seemed to think as he stared straight ahead. Alex used the time to regret her words. Everyone knew the man had been sucked in by Natalie's physical charms; there was no mystery there. And maybe he had mentioned other traits. Truth of the matter was that she'd stopped really listening to him rattle on about Natalie.

Alex was torn from her thoughts by the loud popping sound a gun makes when it's discharged. Instantly, the car swerved. Thorn swore as the car careened toward the shoulder of the highway. As they crossed the four lanes of traffic to get there, other cars braked, horns honked. Alex stopped breathing as they missed one car after another until Thorn managed to maneuver them to a standstill. Traffic continued to whiz by them at breakneck speed as they sat in silence, too stunned for a second to move.

"What happened?" Alex finally managed to say as Thorn got out of the car. He stood by the front bumper, knelt for a second, then reappeared.

"It's a blowout," he said.

"It sounded as though someone shot out your tire," she said, shock now producing a case of chattering teeth and shaking hands. There for a second, she'd thought their trek was about to come to an abrupt, and bloody, end.

"No, it's a nail. Damn! We probably picked it up on that dirt road."

Alexandra hugged herself and tried to look composed. The next thing she knew, Thorn had opened her door and whisked her out of the car, taking her toward a fence as far from the traffic as he could. He enfolded her in a warm hug, his cheek against the top of her head, his arms strong and protective.

"It's okay, it's okay," he crooned.

She tried nodding but what she wanted to do was cry. She'd been so scared.

"It's over, we're safe," he continued, adding other soothing sounds that had no form. Gradually she felt the strength in her limbs return.

He lifted her chin with his finger. "You're the one who barely lifted an eyebrow when you got tossed around by that big wave, remember?"

She tried smiling. "Give me a big old hulking wave anytime," she said. "But cars—"

"I know." His voice was soothing, and the thought crossed Alex's mind what a wonderful father he would someday make.

"You okay now?"

She nodded. "Now I just feel like an idiot—"

"Don't be silly. I was scared, too."

"You didn't look it," she said.

He smiled warmly. "I'm a big old he-man. I'm tough and brave and sex starved, all at the same time."

Alex laughed.

"And now I'll go change the tire. You stay here by the fence—"

"No," she said, regaining composure. "I'll help you."

"Now, Alexandra—"

"I said I'll help."

He studied her for a second. "You're something else, you know that?"

Unsure what he meant, she bit her lip and waited.

"Just when I think I know you, you say or do something that startles me. You have a lot of guts, don't you?"

"I don't know—"

"Well, I do. Come on, you can help if you like. Just don't stand too near the traffic and get run over, okay?"

"Wouldn't think of it," she said as they started back toward the car. "We're already late reaching Natalie. Think how much time it would take to scrape me off the pavement—"

He turned back and glared at her. "*That's* not even funny," he said.

She laughed again.

As they entered the Red Swan Hotel, Alex thanked her lucky stars, and her sister, for her new improved wardrobe. Gone were the parachute pants and bright sweatshirt, and in their place, blue-gray shorts and a coordinating blouse made from rough silk. Vicky had said that none of her clothes fit anymore, that Alex could take her time returning them. With her hair neatly tucked into a well-pinned roll and makeup minimizing her discolored eye, Alex felt as though she at least no longer stood out like a mongrel at a dog show.

Thorn was in the same clothes he'd worn the night before. There was a slight streak of grease on his knee she hadn't noticed until that moment, attained, probably, when he knelt to fix the tire, a job which turned out to be a nightmare event considering the speed and close proximity of the passing cars. Still, even with people jostling by him wearing designer dresses and thousand-dollar suits, he looked right at home.

Why was that? He was such a contradiction, a cowboy with a Mercedes, seemingly equally at home on a Boogie board or a horse, mingling with ranch hands and millionaires, suave one moment, charmingly down-home the next.

He wasted no time perusing those around him, she noticed, just marched across the fifty or so acres of plush red carpeting, past the splattering two-story waterfall that was graced with several crystal swans, right on up to the desk.

An Asian woman with the prettiest smile Alex had ever seen asked how she could help him. He asked, with the force born of five days of frustration, in which room were Gerald and Jasmine Blackwell. She kissed him off with another lovely smile and offered to ring their room for him.

Alex smirked at the floor as Thorn talked his way out of calling Blackwell's room. "I'll leave them a note," he finally said.

"I'll ring their room and you can leave an electronic note on their telephone," the clerk said sweetly. "We've found it much more convenient for our guests than written notes, which they may or may not collect."

"Let me think about what I want to say," Thorn said, and steered Alex to the circular bench by the waterfall.

"What kind of note were you going to leave?" Alex demanded.

"I don't know, something noncommittal, anything just so I could see which cubbyhole she put it in."

"They don't have cubbyholes, at least not anywhere I could see."

"They don't? I guess I just assumed."

"I think you watch too much television."

"I don't watch *any* television," he grumbled as he stood. "Well, okay, that didn't work. Now we go to plan B."

"Which is?"

As he pulled her to her feet, he said, "We find someone to bribe."

"And how do we do that?"

"Look for someone young and inexperienced."

Chuckling, Alex added, "With shifty eyes?"

"It couldn't hurt."

"I can't even imagine where we'll start."

"We'll start with room service," he said. "If I know Natalie, she's been ordering her breakfast in bed every morning. Wait, I have it. We'll use an interhotel phone to place a call to room service. You can pretend to be Natalie."

"Oh, joy."

"Come on, Alexandra. We're so close now, I can practically taste it."

Capitulating, Alex used the phone in a remote corner of the lobby and called room service. "My name is Jasmine Blackwell, I'm a guest here, and I'd like a pot of tea, my usual kind, sent at once," she said. She went on to explain why she was calling from the lobby, and how she'd forgotten the room number, how she always just followed Gerald around and he was in the bar right that second, but a pot of tea in their room when they arrived would be heavenly.

"Did they buy it?" Thorn asked as she hung up.

"I think so. And Thorn, they called me *Mrs.* Blackwell."

He was silent for a second. "Well," he finally said as he ran a hand through his hair. "I never really thought she was traveling around like this with her father, did you?"

"No," Alex admitted. "What do we do now?"

"Now we find the kitchen and keep an eye on the service elevator."

Which they did. It was simply a smaller elevator located around the corner from the regular ones reserved for high-paying guests. Within twenty minutes, a young man in a white jacket approached, carrying a tray with one porcelain pot of tea and two matching cups. He got on the elevator. Thorn stepped in with him quickly, followed by Alex. Though the man seemed surprised by their presence, he was too polite to say anything about their being on the wrong elevator.

He pushed the button for the fourth floor. "And which

floor do you need, sir?'' he asked as his hand hovered near the buttons.

"What a coincidence. We're going to the fourth floor, too. Boy, that tea sure smells good."

The man nodded. Alex felt her heart flip-flop. This was it. She was acutely aware of the growing sense of tenseness in Thorn's body. She herself felt a mixture of emotions, running the gauntlet from fear to anxiety to a creeping sense of sadness she couldn't explain. It was almost over, just the fireworks left. Almost over...

The door slid open to reveal an exceptionally wide hallway carpeted in red, the wallpaper covered with swans. They got off before the man with the tray and lingered near a door close to the elevator, both of them watching as the man walked down the hall. He stopped near the end and rapped on a door across from an abandoned maid's cart.

"Showtime," Thorn said, grasping Alex's elbow and steering her toward the waiter.

She fleetingly wondered why she was walking down the hall with a man she'd known less than a week. She fleetingly wondered if she should be feeling panic and discomfort at the thought of the impending showdown when the truth was, she felt slightly exhilarated.

Thinking was pointless now. It was too late to question motives or methods, the time was upon them. She sensed Thorn looking down at her, and she cast him a blinding smile.

The room service waiter knocked again as they approached. Alex glanced through the open door across the hall and saw a large woman with hair as red as the apron that was wrapped around her ample body. The woman was in the process of coming out into the hall. Thorn noticed her, too, and he took Alex a couple of steps past Natalie's door and pretended to look for his key.

"You ain't gonna find them in there, Georgie," the woman said with a snort.

"But they ordered tea, leastways, she did," the man with the tray answered.

"I don't care what she ordered. They was in that room most of the day and I don't need to tell you what they was up to. But they're gone now."

The man set the tray down in front of the door. "Maybe they're coming right back—"

He was interrupted by a friendly laugh. "Not likely. She was dressed in diamonds and a long cape and I heard her going on and on about the Space Needle and dinner and champagne. Must have left here thirty minutes ago."

About this time, in unison, the maid and the waiter seemed to notice that Alex and Thorn were hanging on their every word. Thorn swore loudly, claimed he'd left his key in the car and stomped back toward the elevator leaving Alex to mumble, "Men!" and scramble after him.

It was a relief to step out of the hotel back onto the crowded sidewalk. They stood staring at each other for several seconds.

"This means we have to go to the Space Needle," Thorn said.

"Or wait in the lobby for them to return," Alex offered.

"No, no, I played that game once before. Remember? No, if they're at the Space Needle, that's where we're going. Or at least it's where *I'm* going."

"Does that mean you're ready to strike out on your own?" Was he asking her to leave? And if he was, why was she feeling startled rather than glad? Well, thank goodness she'd thought to borrow money from Vicky so she wasn't totally dependent.

Still staring at her, he sighed. "What do you think?"

"I don't know what to think," she told him honestly.

"Well, the answer is, hell, no, I don't *want* you to leave. I'm hoping you'll stay until the bitter end—you know that. But I do realize I've asked you to do some pretty strange things and you might be getting sick of me. How's your wrist?''

Alex hadn't thought about her wrist for quite some time—a definite improvement. ''My wrist is fine and I'm in this now,'' she told him with conviction. ''For me, it's kind of like stopping to watch a building burn to the ground. There's nothing you can do to stop the fire, but it's very hard to turn away. Besides, I'm on vacation and I'm hungry and I've never been to the Space Needle before. You buying?''

''Anything your little heart desires,'' he told her and slinging his arm around her shoulder, began walking toward the car. Alex realized the gesture was meant to convey partnership and camaraderie. But for her, the weight of his arm brought to mind other times when they'd been close, and the feelings she was suddenly swamped with were bittersweet.

Of course, now it was perfectly obvious who the fool was!

The Space Needle looked like a flying saucer sitting atop several hundred feet of metal framework. By the time they parked the car and rode the elevator to the top where the revolving restaurant was located, it was the height of the dinner hour. Thorn accomplished a well-placed bribe, and their name was moved toward the top of the list. Alex watched all this with fascination because she'd never before been with someone who had actually slipped a maître d' a fifty-dollar bill, and it was interesting in a clinical kind of way. Apparently, money talked.

Well, of course it did. In fact, judging from Natalie's behavior, money didn't just talk, it screamed and yelled and stamped its feet, too.

It crossed Alex's mind to wonder how Thorn would confront Natalie in such a crowded place. A scene here would be witnessed by dozens of people; there was no way around it. She glanced up at Thorn, who looked totally at ease.

"You wait in line, I'll reconnoiter the place," he said softly.

"Don't you dare talk to her until you come back and get me," she warned him.

He said, "I promise," and disappeared into the throng.

He was back by the time a waiter had appeared to show them to a table. Their progress was slow as Thorn stopped to examine the face of every likely looking woman they passed. Alex tried to ignore him.

The day was growing old. Long slanting shafts of sunlight blanketed Seattle, which was spread out below them in a breathtaking panorama backed by the majestic peak of Mount Rainier. Alex fought the irrational desire to be there with Thorn on a date, alone, without Natalie dominating both their minds.

"The dining area of the restaurant makes a complete revolution every hour," the waiter told them as they gave their drink orders.

As soon as he was gone, Alex leaned across the table. "You obviously didn't find her."

"I got trapped behind a group of tourists so I didn't even get to look."

Alex opened the menu. "Look at this. They have salmon fixed three different ways. And prawns. I love prawns. Don't you?"

"Sure. Listen, you order me the prawns and you have whatever you like. I see that knot of tourists has moved so I'm going to take a walk round this place and find her."

"Wait. Soup or salad, what kind of dressing, potato or pilaf?"

He was standing, but he leaned down, placing his face close to Alex's ear. "I really don't give a damn. You decide. I'll be back in a few minutes." And then he was gone again.

The restaurant's interior was darker than the world outside, its romantic, individual tables lit by small candles. Alex sat alone, refusing to let her thoughts wander far afield. They went without her permission. Damn Thorn! Why had he run off so quickly? Couldn't he stay and order his own dinner?

Come off it, her subconscious whispered. *What you're really irritated about is the fact that he left you alone. What you really want is for him to be content gazing lovingly into your eyes!* Alex looked over the sea of heads, searching for a sight of him, but the curvature of the restaurant cut her field of vision. She told her subconscious to shut up.

The waiter showed up with two chilled glasses of white wine. "Put them both over here," she said, tapping a spot by her plate.

"Shall I bring something else for the gentleman?" he asked as he set both glasses down in front of Alex.

"Oh, I don't think so. He's not here, is he?"

The man looked unmoved, as though irritated customers were part and parcel of his job. Alex shrugged. "I'm sorry, I'm just a little miffed with the gentleman. It happens, you know."

"Oh, don't I know it?" he mumbled, adding, after a slight pause, "Will he be returning?"

"Probably. Just bring us two of the prawn dinners. You choose whatever else goes on the plate, I don't care."

The waiter wrote something down on his pad and faded away.

Alex stared out at the slowly spinning world. As daylight failed, lights began twinkling on around the city, one after the other. Enchanting, she thought. She took a sip of wine and searched again for Thorn. Where was he? Why was it taking him so long to circumnavigate the place? He wouldn't find Natalie and tell her off by himself, would he? He'd better not!

* * *

The restaurant was dark and confusing. The floor was multileveled and the doorways leading from the middle to the various areas on the perimeter were crowded with people. Thorn moved as quickly as he could, but the place was set up for ambience and privacy, not for tracking someone down.

He had the feeling he'd made it about halfway around when he heard a woman laugh. The sound hit him like a rock in the gut, punched him painfully in the heart, rattled him between the eyes. *He knew that laugh....*

He followed it to a table on the higher level, a table hidden away and private. A man with long white hair caught in a low ponytail sat on one side of the table, his hands extended to the woman seated opposite. He was talking. She had placed her hands in his and was favoring the man with throaty, sexy laughter.

Thorn ducked behind a convenient post, then carefully edged out a ways until he could stare at Jasmine Blackwell, a.k.a. Natalie Dupree. She was dressed in black velvet, her white shoulders bare. She was overdressed for the restaurant, but that was Natalie. Her lips were bright red, making her teeth, in comparison, look as white as new snow. She held her head slightly to the left, her focus totally devoted to the tanned man holding her hands.

How well he recalled that look, that laugh, that intense concentration that cut straight to a man's gut. For one vivid fire-eating second, he was blasted with jealousy, and he closed his eyes against the pain. But it passed. In fact, it passed so quickly he was left dumbfounded.

He opened his eyes and stared at her again, mesmerized by her actions. A performance—that was the way her moves struck him now, seen as they were from a distance and through the lens of experience. An actress playing a part, saying the right things, blinking, fluttering eyelashes, even breathing on cue. She had her performance down pat;

hell, it would fool anyone. The only reason he recognized it as an act was that it was exactly the way she had behaved with him.

And then she shifted position ever so slightly and the light glittered off what she wore around her neck. A sapphire necklace, each stone set in white gold and circled with diamonds. A unique piece of jewelry, valued in the thousands, but actually, at least to Thorn, beyond price.

His grandmother's necklace. Good heavens, how had he managed to forget he'd given Natalie that necklace!

Hands balled into fists at his side, he took a step toward her, then retreated. He couldn't confront her without Alexandra, he'd given his word. But he wanted to—oh, how he wanted to! For some time he stood there, racked with indecision, vacillating between marching up and pouring champagne over their heads and going back to collect Alexandra.

As he watched, Natalie plucked a red rose from the vase on the table and drew it across Gerald Blackwell's cheek before leaning across the table and brushing her lips against Blackwell's lips. A waitress interrupted this charming little love scene by depositing dinner plates in front of them. Lobster, of course. Natalie was a one-woman threat to the lobster population of the world.

Well, hell, they weren't going anywhere for a couple of minutes! Thorn turned his back on them and made his way to the center of the restaurant, exiting near his own table.

Something funny happened to him as he approached it. Alexandra was staring outside, her back to him, and he suddenly had the overwhelming desire for her to turn, for her eyes to meet his. It wasn't just that he wanted her to notice him so they could go find Natalie again, either. He wasn't sure what it was, just that he yearned to see Alexandra Williams's eyes.

As if she sensed him there, she did turn, and her blue gaze swamped him.

He sat down opposite her, which wasn't what he had planned to do, but he felt the need to sit.

She flashed him a dazzling smile. "Well, well, looky who finally came back!" she said. Her voice sounded different to Thorn. Now that he really stared at her, her eyes looked different, too. Softer, bigger.

"You missed the salad," she continued. "Oh, well, lettuce is lettuce, right? But the wine, now, that was very tasty, very tasty indeed. Charnonay...wait, wait, Chardobay. No, that's not it."

"Chardonnay?" he suggested as he took in the two empty glasses by her plate.

"That's it."

He finally noticed his dinner sitting on the table. She'd almost finished hers.

"I just love prawns. Don't you, Thorn Powell? And these are really yummy." She plucked a prawn from her plate and waved it at him. "Know what I think? I think it's all these little crumb things they stick on the outside." With her final word, she lost hold of the prawn, which flew into space and disappeared into the shadows. As though completely unaware of it, she put both elbows on the table, propped her chin in her hands and peered intently into his eyes. "What do you think, Mr. Powell?"

"Good heavens, Alexandra, I think you're drunk!"

Her hands were in motion again. "What a silly thing to say!"

He caught her hand with his. "Honey, we don't have time for this. I found her!"

"Little Natalie, come home, come home," she sang with an enigmatic smile.

"How much wine did you drink?"

She looked perplexed. "Just two. Yours and mine. But you weren't here. You were off searching for Natalie."

"Do you drink very often?"

Ignoring him, she produced a wicked little smile. "Poor

little Natalie, lost like a ship out at sea without a compass. Tragic, isn't it?''

He smiled at her. She was awfully cute. Drunk, but cute. He said, ''You stay here and I'll go talk to Natalie. And then we'll drive back to your sister's house. Don't drink any more wine and don't fall asleep.''

She tore the napkin from her lap and tossed it on her plate. ''Nothin' doin'. I'm going with you.''

''I would rather you stayed—''

She stood swiftly and swayed. ''Lead on, McDuff.''

He grabbed her elbow and steadied her. ''Okay, okay, just slow down.''

Somehow they got back to the center of the place, and then exited where Natalie and Blackwell should have been. The restaurant had rotated farther than he anticipated, however, and he looked around in confusion. At last, he decided not to waste any more time retracing his steps, and pulled a tipsy Alexandra along behind him.

And then he stopped abruptly. Alexandra bumped into his back. He heard her giggle, felt her push around his side. ''Whatsa matter?'' she asked.

Thorn didn't answer. He was staring at a small table, vacant except for two lobster carcasses, one of which was draped with an abandoned red rose.

A waitress appeared to clear the table and noticed them standing there, gawking at the remains of someone else's dinner. ''May I help you, sir?''

Thorn realized they were blocking traffic. He pulled Alexandra against him, staring at the waitress while he searched for words.

Alexandra said, her words slightly slurred, ''It's like this. We're looking for some people. He's a really good-looking guy with long white hair, and she's a witch. Well, not really a witch, not like Samantha on that television show. What I mean is that she's a—'' She immediately slapped her hand over her mouth and added, ''Oops.''

Thorn sighed. "You'll have to excuse my...wife. She wanted to say hello to her...sister who was dining at this table with her...companion...but by the time we got here she'd left—"

"Mr. and Mrs. Blackwell?"

Thorn instructed his face to remain passive. "That's right."

"They've been here two nights in a row now. Great tipper, your brother-in-law. Nice guy."

Alexandra pulled on Thorn's arm. When he looked down at her, she said, "You notice how she didn't say Natalie was nice? That's 'cause she isn't."

The waitress furled her brow. "And you say she's *your* sister?"

"We've never been close," Alexandra mumbled.

"My wife was hoping to take this opportunity to patch things up."

"She killed our parents," Alexandra volunteered.

Thorn immediately turned her around and gazed deep into her eyes. "Now, honey, let's not exaggerate." He looked back at the waitress. "We'll catch up with them at the hotel." He started walking, Alexandra held tightly against his side.

"Sir?"

He turned to find the waitress looking totally baffled. "The Blackwells told me they were catching a train tonight. As a matter of fact, that's why they had to leave early, to check out of their hotel and drive to the train station for the 9:35."

"You've been very helpful," Thorn mumbled as he once again began moving toward the exit.

Alexandra leaned around behind him, calling out, "Thanks so much!"

"Come on," he said.

She planted her small body like a rock in the middle of a stream. "We're leaving? I haven't had any dessert."

Thorn smiled at the couple at a window table who had turned to watch them, then gave his full attention to Alexandra. "I'm sorry," he murmured, "but we have to hurry."

She batted her eyelashes. "Sweets for the sweet?"

"I think you've had enough of everything for one evening," he grumbled, and almost lifting her, continued back to their table.

By the time he settled their bill and got Alexandra planted in the car, it was dangerously close to nine o'clock. He had to forgo trying to catch Natalie and Blackwell at the hotel and drive directly to the Amtrak station. Their waiter had given them directions, and while Alexandra grew increasingly quiet, Thorn drove like a maniac.

The thought crossed his mind that this whole thing was beginning to get drastically out of hand.

Chapter Eight

The train was pulling out of the station as they squealed to a stop outside the depot. For a few seconds, Thorn sat behind the wheel and stared at the retreating lights, listened to the retreating whistle and swore under his breath.

He glanced down at Alexandra, who sat in her bucket seat, head thrown back against the support, body totally relaxed. She was asleep, and though he should be annoyed with her for botching up the Space Needle, he couldn't find it in his heart. She'd been so kind, really, so patient, such a good sport, and she hadn't slept well in days. It was only natural that she'd sooner or later let down her guard, though he could have wished it had happened later rather than sooner.

But boy, it sure didn't take much alcohol to send this woman over the top!

The outside light bathed her face and he carefully reached over and brushed a stray curl away from her eyes. She made a sweet little sound and turned her face toward his hand, her lips touching his palm for a second before he made himself withdraw his hand. For a second, he recalled the experience in the Space Needle restaurant when he'd longed for her to look at him, really look at him. It was crazy in retrospect, but at the time, he'd felt the need for her gaze like a thirsty man craves water, or a tired man, a bed.

No bed for them, not tonight. He put up the top of the car and locked all the doors. Alexandra slept through the whole procedure. He went into the station and found a helpful employee who gave him a schedule and suggested the next best place to catch up with the train would be Portland.

Thorn inwardly groaned at the thought of another five hours of driving, but he stoically returned to the car and let himself in the door. Alexandra still slept. He studied the schedule, finally admitting that the station clerk had been right, Portland was the logical place to check. Frustrated, he dumped the brochure onto the floor and took off.

The radio, turned low, kept him company. He set the speed control for five miles per hour over the speed limit, then clicked his mind into the same automatic gear. The only time it kicked out was when he recognized the exit for Alexandra's sister's house and he briefly considered turning off and leaving Alexandra with Vicky. And then it was too late—the exit was gone, and he realized he'd never really seriously thought about stopping, that it was all an act, a sham. He wanted her with him. She was somehow tied up in this blasted affair, tied up with him. *For better or worse, they were in this thing together.*

The words had a familiar ring to them that made him squirm.

He arrived at the Amtrak station before the schedule said the train was due, which, considering his luck over the past few days, seemed like a miracle. He wasn't going to take any chances. As Alexandra was still asleep, he locked her in the car again and went into the station where he bought a ticket; it was the only way the train people said he could get aboard. Good enough, then. If Natalie didn't get off, he'd get on. Time to wrap up this little fiasco.

When he went back to the car he found Alexandra rubbing the sleep from her eyes.

"Are you okay?" he asked as he slid into his seat.

She narrowed her eyes and stared at him. "Where are we?"

"Portland."

"But Seattle—"

"Is behind us. They got on a train so we followed them. In fact, the train is due to arrive here any minute."

"Oh, goody," she groaned.

"You're just grumpy because you have a hangover."

"I never have hangovers. I'm grumpy because I need to use the ladies' room."

"Be my guest. Right through those doors. But the train is due back and I may have to board, so if you don't want to be locked out of the car—"

"I'll hurry," she snapped, and slammed the door after her.

Within minutes, she returned, two cold cans of cola in her hands. She got back in the car and gave him one of the soft drinks.

"Thanks. I wish I'd thought to get you a cold drink."

"I wish you had, too," she said before taking a healthy swallow.

He leaned toward her. "What do you mean by that?"

"Nothing."

"Don't cop out on me. What do you mean?"

She bit her bottom lip, which he recognized as a sign that she was contemplating whether or not to say what she was thinking. Experience told him that she'd blurt something out in a second or two and that she'd probably almost instantly regret it even though there would be the bite of truth to her words. He both wanted her to say whatever it was that was bothering her, and wanted her to keep it to herself.

"I mean that you never think of me as anything but a Tonto to your Long Ranger."

He laughed. He couldn't help himself. She looked hurt and indignant and he was sorry about that, but it just struck him as funny.

"Stop laughing," she growled.

"I'm sorry."

"Then stop!"

"Okay, okay. Listen, honey, you're right, I have been insensitive—"

"And don't call me that," she interrupted.

"Don't call you what?"

"'Honey.' I am not your honey."

"I know—"

"You've done it three times now."

"No—"

"Yes, you have. Twice in the Space Needle and once right now."

"You were drunk—"

She smiled a smile that wasn't really a smile and said, "I admit I was a little *tipsy* but I do remember everything that happened, so spare me the details."

"But I wasn't—"

"I hear a whistle."

And so did he. He put the unopened can on the floor as he opened his door. Alexandra got out the car, as well, and both of them stared down the tracks.

The train rumbled to a halt thirty feet in front of them. It didn't take long for people to appear on the platform, which was actually just a piece of pavement painted to separate the tracks from the buildings.

They waited as dozens of people disembarked, as dozens of others rushed forward to greet and hug. A few minutes passed and then more people came forward, people boarding the train for the trip that would continue south.

"I didn't see either one of them, did you?" Thorn asked as he came around the car.

She shook her head, wincing as though the act made her uncomfortable.

He stared at the crowds as goodbyes were exchanged, then he looked down at Alexandra. "I guess I have to get aboard to look for her. I'd better go now so I can get off before they leave."

"But it looks as though they're leaving any second."

He checked his watch against the numbers from the schedules, which swam inside his brain. "I have ten minutes. It's my only choice. This means you'll miss all the action—"

"It's okay," she told him with the first genuine smile he'd seen her produce since she woke up. "I can't see that there's any other way. Go."

He took a step away, then turned back. "Oh, hell, everyone else is doing it," he said quickly before leaning down and kissing her. He'd intended it to be brief, one quick peck and he'd disappear into the throng before she could chastise him. Instead, he found himself lingering, savoring the delicate softness of her lips, the hubbub around him all but forgotten. It returned in force when they simultaneously parted. Before Thorn could think of anything to say, the crowd jostled him, moving him toward the train and the boarding line. His last sight of Alexandra revealed startled eyes and a hand raised to her mouth.

That's when he realized his lips were tingling too.

"Ticket, sir?"

As he handed his ticket to the porter, he cautioned himself to put thoughts of Alexandra aside. *Concentrate on finding Natalie.*

Alexandra watched Thorn disappear into the train with the funny feeling she'd never see him again. As her hand drifted away from her lips, she decided it was the kiss, so like a goodbye, so unexpected...and so wonderful. How long had she dreamed about what it would be like to kiss Thorn Powell? Longer than she cared to admit, that was for sure. She had no idea why he had chosen this time and place to unwittingly fulfill her fantasy; she suspected it was an impulsive gesture on his part, all but forgotten as he moved through the train looking for Natalie. Question was, could she forget the thrill that had raced through her body when his delicious lips touched hers? Did she even want to?

Numb with fatigue and with a splitting headache, she got back into the car, cursing the wine she'd drunk at the Space Needle. Apparently, she still wasn't much of a drinker. She fished around in Vicky's borrowed purse for the aspirin her sister had given her for her wrist. After swallowing the pills, she examined her arm and decided it was almost healed. As she was curious about what her black eye looked like, she twisted the rearview mirror to take a look at herself. She studied her own face only briefly before catching sight of someone else who was passing behind the car. Good grief, long white hair, tanned skin!

She turned in the seat in time to see Natalie and Gerald Blackwell approaching a limousine. Natalie was in a black dress that brushed her ankles, a dark satin cape draped over her shoulders. As they stood by the fancy car, she reached up and touched Blackwell's cheek. He caught her hand and brought it to his lips and they stood like that, staring at each other.

Thorn! she screamed without opening her mouth.

Where was he?

In answer, the train blew a whistle and began rolling away.

She searched the platform for Thorn's familiar figure but he wasn't there, which meant he was still on that train!

Alex twisted around in her seat again and saw that Natalie had already entered the limo and that Gerald was following.

Alex quickly got out of the car and ran around to the driver's door. She got in behind the wheel and wasted precious seconds adjusting the seat so she could reach the pedals. As the limousine slowly began making its way toward the exit, she backed the car out of the parking space and followed, sure that at any moment, Thorn would come running up to the door and take over.

He didn't come.

She had to dig around in her purse for money to pay the parking attendant, and still he didn't come.

He's gone, he's on that train, she told herself as she heard another whistle and the sound of the train gaining speed. With one final fruitless glance behind her, she rolled through the exit and got behind the limo.

What am I doing! she asked herself as they merged onto a busy street. She was following Natalie, of course. She'd been doing that for—what? five days now? No, it was well after midnight so make it six days. It was like a reflex now: follow Natalie.

She tailed the limo onto the freeway and then drove for fifteen or twenty minutes until it became apparent they were headed for the airport. Thorn, of course, was at the back of her mind. Had he really been on the train or had he disembarked without her seeing and ducked inside the station for a moment? She hadn't had time to make a rational decision; it had been either follow or stay. What if Thorn had had his thirty seconds with Natalie and it was all over?

She hit her fist against the steering wheel and kept going. No sense in second-guessing now. If Thorn was waiting for her, he would just have to wait a few minutes longer. And if he wasn't waiting...what then?

He'd been right; she had been grumpy. The travel was beginning to catch up with her, that was all. The sleepless nights, the irregular meals and the tension of being near a man who didn't know she existed were taking their toll. That and the wine. She inwardly cringed as she recalled the Space Needle. While she did remember most of what happened, some of her conversation was lost in a fog. Maybe that was good. She only hoped she hadn't made too big a fool of herself.

The limo came to a stop outside of the Reno Air terminal. As Alex pulled to the curb and watched, the driver opened the rear passenger door and Gerald Blackwell emerged. He leaned back inside and helped Natalie onto the sidewalk while the driver retrieved two suitcases from the trunk and carried them to an airport baggage station.

Alex made the loop back to the freeway, and eventually to Portland, both amazed and grateful that she didn't once get lost.

The Amtrak station was deserted when she got there. Still, she walked along the platform, stopping to look through the station windows in the hope of finding Thorn. No such luck—not even an employee to ask where the train went next!

She went back to the car, riddled with indecision about what to do. Thorn's unopened can of soda had been rolling around on the floor for the past twenty miles, driving her nuts, so she leaned down to retrieve it. She found a folder on the floor beside the can and turned on the interior light to see what it was.

An Amtrak time schedule! Quickly she flipped through the brochure until she found the right page, and running her finger down the list, found the next town after Portland at which the train stopped.

Her next move was to find an open gas station, fuel the car and buy a map. This accomplished, and the route set in her mind, she once again took off, hoping against hope that Thorn had been on the train and that he would have the good sense to get off at the very first opportunity. She didn't allow herself to think about the possibility that he'd

talked his way off the train before it left Portland and that
even now, he was walking the dark streets toward the station where he thought she—and his car—awaited him.

It was after midnight when she drove into Albany,
Oregon, and finally found the train station. It, too, was dark
and deserted, and Alex felt her heart slip down into her
stomach. Now what?

The question was answered almost immediately as a figure rose from a bench off to the side of the building and
started toward her. The man hadn't taken three steps before
Alexandra knew it was Thorn. Though he was still too far
away and too heavily shadowed to see clearly, there was,
nevertheless, an unmistakable quality to his walk that announced it was him as clearly as if his face was flooded
with sunlight. She got out of the car and waited, mesmerized by the sight of him coming closer, his features growing
more distinct as he covered the distance between them.

"I can't even begin to tell you how glad I am that you're
here," he called out.

She was so relieved to have found him that the laughter
bubbled up inside her and spilled through her lips.

"Who would have thought that my kissing you goodbye
would really mean goodbye?" he continued as he finally
reached her side. He took her in his arms and hugged her.

A lover's hug—that was what she craved. Not this
wholesome embrace that spoke of relief at being found. He
lifted her from her feet and turned once, then returned her
to earth.

"They weren't on the train," he said, holding her at
arm's length, "unless they were in a sleeping car, which is
a distinct possibility, but I bribed a guy who said they
weren't."

Alex worked at ignoring the feel of his hands clasped on
her arms and the look of his eyes in a world of black and
white and a zillion shades of gray. She worked even harder
at forgetting what it had felt like when he kissed her, how

for just an instant, it had seemed the two of them had connected as man and woman in a place out of time. She thought briefly of flinging herself back into his arms, feigning cold or fatigue, anything just to be close to him again.

He regarded her with concern. "Are you okay?"

"I'm fine."

"Listen, I'm sorry I haven't been considerate of your feelings and that I laughed at you before and that I called you 'honey'—"

"Please," she begged, embarrassed. "I'm the one who's sorry."

"You have no reason to be. I'm the clod."

She smiled at his seriousness. "Okay, you're the clod. Now, stop apologizing so I can tell you what I found out when I followed them—"

"You what!"

"They got off the train and into a limo, which I tailed to the Portland airport. That's what took me so long. Anyway, they seemed to be going to Reno. There was no way I could be absolutely positive but the limo driver checked their bags with Reno Air."

He nodded briskly. "That figures. Natalie has a thing for Reno." He kissed Alex's forehead before adding, "Clever of you to follow them, Alexandra."

"That's me, the clever one," she mumbled.

"Well, hop in the car, we'd better get going."

She didn't bother arguing. She didn't point out that she'd agreed to go only as far as Seattle and it had come and gone. She didn't remind him that this was his quest, not hers, or that she was tired and in need of a shower—again. She didn't even suggest he travel to Reno via the interstate, which would be the long way around but would mean he could drop her off at her place in Cottage Grove on the way and go on by himself. She said only, "Do you want me to drive?"

"No, you must be bushed. I caught a few winks over there on the bench. I'll drive. Let's go."

So, once again they were enclosed in a car, traveling at night, the sky overhead illuminated by the moon, the stars faded but beautiful. Alex didn't protest when he cut off the interstate highway to take a route over the Cascade Mountain range. The dashboard clock was persistently rude about flashing the waning night's hours away, and she struggled to stay awake to help keep Thorn alert as he drove the winding mountain roads.

He pulled into a rest stop around 3:00 a.m.

She looked over at him as he parked the car out near the trucks. "Do you want me to drive now?"

He turned off the engine and yawned. "No," he finally said. "You've been dropping off to sleep for the past hour or so."

"No I haven't—"

"Yes, you have. Anyway, I think we both need a few hours' rest or we're going to kill ourselves."

Alex looked around the dark lot, taking in the hulking shapes of trucks and the long combination of cars and trailers. "Here?"

"Sure, why not?"

"But where will we sleep?"

He moved his hand down near his door and his seat suddenly reclined almost to a horizontal position. "Right here," he said. "Go on, try yours."

"It's going to get cold, you know. At this elevation, as soon as the car cools off, it's going to be like an icebox in here."

He put his seat back up and got out of the car. Alex joined him. The night was chilly and she shivered. He opened the trunk and looked through his suitcase, but Alex could see that he'd packed for the tropics and his wardrobe didn't include sweaters and blankets.

"You are cold," he said as he wrapped a big arm around her shoulders.

Alex leaned against him. She told herself it was because she was cold and he was warm.

He looked down at her, then back up at the sky. "Will you look at all those stars," he said.

She gazed past his head. The sky was darker now as the moon had sunk lower toward the horizon. The sky was littered with bright dots and Alex felt her breath catch at the sight of them.

"I love the stars," he said, his voice very soft beside her ear. He pointed heavenward and added, "See that little group right there? That's the Pleiades."

"The seven daughters of Atlas," she said.

He looked down at her again. "You know about the constellations?"

"A little. I've always been fascinated with the stars. I use to sleep on a deck Dad built above our garage. Vicky hated it up there, but I loved it. I had a book on mythology that I'd read with my flashlight. That's how I learned the stories. The Pleiades were seven sisters who were placed among the stars to save them from the pursuit of Orion."

Thorn looked where she pointed. "Really?"

"That's right. He was a giant-size hunter who was eventually slain by Artemis."

"I didn't know any of this," Thorn said.

Alex smiled at the memories of the huge black sky and the stars that had been like actors on a stage. She said, "I'd go to sleep counting falling stars."

His smile deepened. "I like to lay out in the fields at night and stare up at the sky and do the same thing."

"Aren't you afraid a cow might step on you?"

He laughed. "I chose which field I lay in with extreme care."

Alex gazed back into space. "It must be wonderful having so much land, so much freedom. I live in a small apartment. I can't even have a cat. My yard consists of about five square feet of concrete where I put two chairs and a barbecue so I can entertain.''

"And just who do you entertain?" he asked.

She shrugged. "Friends."

"Male-type friends?"

A soft chuckle escaped her lips. "One or two."

"I bet. You probably have them lined up at the door."

She brought her gaze back to his face, which was turned to study her. "Not really."

"Why not? A woman as pretty as you are—"

"I'm not pretty—"

"Oh, come off it. You're adorable."

"Adorable and pretty aren't quite the same thing," she said quickly, wishing he'd chosen just about any other word in the English language to describe her.

"Maybe not, but some men really like adorable women."

Did *he?* That's what she wanted to know, but suddenly his focus had returned to the trunk. He touched the bag Vicky had loaned Alex. "Did your sister send along any warm clothes?"

"No." Both of their gazes rested next on a huge bundle of yellow silk.

Thorn sighed. "I guess we could use that thing."

"Well, at least I'd get some use out of it."

He took the maid-of-honor dress out of the trunk and they returned to the car. Once both their seats were reclined, they spread the silky dress over their prone bodies.

"Good night, Alexandra," he said.

She murmured good-night.

For several minutes, she lay there and tried to relax, but her mind jumped around. There were so many uncomfortable things she didn't want to contemplate—things having to do with motives and repercussions and the future—that it took mental gymnastics to avoid bumping into them. Her head was suddenly a very crowded place.

Seattle seemed light-years away and yet it was only hours in the past. It also seemed as though she'd known Thorn for most of her life and yet it had only been days.

"Are you asleep?" he whispered.

"No."

"Me neither."

She didn't point out that this was obvious. "Are you comfortable?"

"Pretty much. How about you? Cold?"

"A little," she admitted.

A rustle of silk was followed by the touch of his hand. "Move closer," he said softly.

There was a small matter of an emergency brake that separated the seats, but Alex scooted as close to the middle of the car as she could. He draped his arm across her body.

When he spoke, she was surprised at how close his head was to hers. "Is that better?"

"Yes," she managed to whisper.

"Tell me about your male friends," he said.

She turned her face to his. He was so near, she couldn't take in all his features with one glance so she addressed herself to his delicious lips. "What do you want to know?"

"What did the last one look like?"

"You and your preoccupation with looks."

"You know how *shallow* I am."

"Oh, that. Now listen, Thorn—"

"Humor me. Tell me what the guy looked like. Or wait, was he a real dog? Is that it?"

"I'll have you know Gary was a very good-looking fellow. He had lots of blond hair, lazy blue eyes and a wicked little grin."

"So why didn't you marry him?"

She smiled in the dark. "Not everyone marries a person just because they're attracted to them, Thorn."

"Like me. Is what you're trying to say?"

She didn't answer, and he was silent long enough that Alex began to wonder if she'd offended him. At last he took a deep breath. "Gary wasn't the man you wanted to marry, so you broke it off with him?"

"No. I broke up with him because his eyes weren't the only lazy thing about him. He had no ambition, no passion."

"And you admire those traits?"

"Yes."

"I have those traits," he said softly.

"Yes, you do," she answered.

"And yet you laughed at the thought of marrying me."

"That's not what I was laughing at."

"What then?"

It took her several moments to think of an appropriate answer. At last she said, "You and I don't make any sense, that's all. You like your women gorgeous and mysterious and manipulative. I am none of those things."

She felt his fingers touch her chin before they stroked her cheek and ran across her lips. She waited for him to speak, but he didn't say a word. His fingers left her lips and traveled up her face. He traced her brows, gently touched her eyelids, her nose, her ears.

"If I were blind, I'd still know exactly how you look," he said, his voice as warm and soft as his touch. "I'd know you have a lovely little nose and wavy hair and a rosebud mouth. I'd know your skin feels softer than velvet."

Alex stopped breathing. In her head, she heard the declaration he'd made several days before, the one about never trusting his heart to another woman. Now she needed to tell him to stop, she needed to tell him that his touch and his voice weren't enough, that she wanted more, so much more, and he wasn't ready to offer it.

Instead, she kissed his fingers as they lit on her lips. Her hands moved to his face and she closed her eyes as she traced his features. The angular shape of his jaw, the lean cheeks, the soft, full lips. "I'd know about you, too," she whispered. "I'd know you have a strong jaw and a noble nose and that you wore a cowboy hat."

Chuckling softly, he said, "And how would you know I wear a cowboy hat?"

"Do you?"

"Nine-tenths of the time."

"That's how I would know. You'd tell me."

"That's cheating," he said. "Besides, wait a second, how *do* you know I wear a Stetson?"

"I saw it on you when you came into the flower shop," she said. "That and your dusty boots."

"I never even knew you noticed me."

"I noticed you," she admitted, laughing softly at the depth of the understatement. She felt his face move closer, felt the warmth of his breath approaching like a caress. His lips touched hers tentatively at first, but the hesitation was brief.

One kiss, she thought. But he managed to make one kiss melt into another and another until there was no definition between them, just one long, warm, moist encounter. She felt her body begin to respond to his mouth and his hands as he coaxed feelings from her that were new and foreign and totally addictive.

He was half on top of her when, hugging her close, he lay back in his seat, pulling her with him. Their legs were hopelessly entangled in the silk dress, but suddenly Alex found herself staring down at him.

I love you. The thought came to her like words, unspoken, filling her eyes with tears, blurring his features already heavily shadowed and indistinct. She lowered her head until their lips met again. He didn't taste like ripe fruit, he didn't taste like anything she'd ever experienced. He tasted like Thorn Powell, a tantalizing taste she sensed was both unique and unforgettable.

One of his hands cupped the back of her head, pulling her closer and closer as the other deftly undid the buttons on her blouse and slid the garment from her shoulders. She fumbled with his shirt, his skin beneath her fingers like hot embers that didn't burn. And then they were together, his bare chest against hers, shirt open, blouse discarded, just blissful skin against skin. He kissed her throat as he unzipped her shorts. She ran her hands across sculpted muscles, delighting in the feel of him.

She'd wanted this to happen for days; she admitted that now, admitted it and wholeheartedly delighted in it. It felt *right* to kiss him, *right* to have his hands roam her body, *right* to be so close and yet yearn to be closer.

As she wondered how to circumvent the yards and yards of material that impeded access to his zipper, unwanted thoughts popped to the surface of her mind like trapped air bubbles in a pond. She was just about to make love to a man in the front seat of a car at a rest stop, no less! The man was chasing down his runaway bride! The man had vocally declared he was through with love! What was wrong with this picture?

She wanted to grasp his face and force him to look at her. She wanted him to announce that he was ready to abandon this crazy goal, drive back to Cottage Grove and beg her to love him forever. And when they made love, if they made love, she wanted it in a more dignified manner than this.

She wanted to be part of his life and his future, and she wanted him to love her in the same, passionate, devoted way he'd thought he'd loved Natalie, in the same way she was discovering she loved him.

His hand stroked the small of her back, weakening her resolve to stop this dangerous game before it was too late. As he sucked on her ear and began further exploration, she arched away from him and took a series of deep breaths.

Her heart was pounding so hard, she felt as though it must be rocking the car.

He, too, came up for air. "What's wrong?"

It took her a moment to speak. "This is wrong," she said at last.

"No, this isn't wrong," he said playfully, raising his head until their lips met again. She allowed herself this final indulgence. It might well be the last kiss they'd ever share, and she wanted to remember it.

And then she gently pushed on his chest until he softly fell back against his seat.

"I can't make love like this," she said as his eyes gazed deeply into hers.

He stared at her for an eternity, twisting one of her curls around his finger. "I know it's uncomfortable," he finally said. "I wish I had an idea where we could find a hotel or—"

"No, it's not the car, Thorn. It's us."

A long pause was followed with the word, "Us?"

"I'm sorry. I didn't mean to lead you on. I got as carried away as you did, but I can't have sex with a man who is chasing down his wayward bride who happens to be a friend of mine. Or at least, she used to be. I don't know, it's all so confusing. All I'm sure of is that this isn't right. It isn't who I am. I can't make love to a man I don't..."

Her voice trailed off. She'd been about to say that she couldn't make love to a man she didn't love but that hardly fit because her feelings for him all but consumed her. What did fit was that she couldn't make love with a man who didn't love her. She couldn't bring herself to say that because she had the feeling he'd protest, caught up in the moment as he was, and she knew the truth: Thorn Powell was still obsessed with Natalie Dupree.

"So you want to stop?" he asked, his lips so close, his words were puffs of warm air against her face.

"No," she croaked. "Yes. Yes."

He ran a shaky hand down her cheek as his eyes stared deeply into hers. Time seemed to stop as the moment between them lengthened and spun away from reality, and then he sighed and broke the spell. With some difficulty, he helped Alex regain her seat, and as she found her blouse and put it on, he got out of the car and walked around for a while. She could barely make out his shape as the inside of the windows were fogged from the passion of a few minutes before, passion that had now dissipated like a drift of petals before a brisk wind, passion she'd killed.

She was reclining in her seat when he returned, internally cursing her convictions, knowing she'd done the right thing, wishing in many ways she hadn't.

He got into the car. "It's chilly enough out there to act like a dry version of a cold shower," he said as he claimed his half of the dress. He put cool fingers against Alex's cheek and looked into her eyes. "I enjoyed it while it lasted," he said softly.

She hadn't known what to expect from him. Anger? Satire? Some kind of pressure to resume where they'd left off? Any of these she could have handled, but somehow his tenderness stabbed her in the heart. "So did I."

As his hand dropped away, she realized that starting right that second, she'd better take care to safeguard her heart. For while Thorn seemed to be in the process of recovery, she was teetering on the brink of critical condition!

Chapter Nine

The sign that stretched across the road leading into town proclaimed Reno to be The Biggest Little City in the World.

Alex had never been to Reno before. Her father liked to gamble but her mother hated it, so while Alex was growing up, they compromised by going to Las Vegas every other year so that Vicky, Alex and their mother could visit with Grandpa while Dad and Grandma played in the casinos. That had all ended years before, and since working at the flower shop, Alex had had precious little extra time or money for extravagances like Reno.

It was a little after noon. Alex looked over at Thorn and found his face reflecting the same bone-weary fatigue she herself felt. The night had been cold and uncomfortable, both physically and emotionally, and they'd given up trying to sleep right after daybreak. They'd stopped briefly for an early lunch. Alex had eaten soup, but for the life of her, she wasn't sure which kind it was or how it had tasted.

He turned onto a side street between two casinos and stopped the car. For a second, both of them sat and watched the throngs of people walking the sidewalks, little margarine containers of coins clasped securely in their hands as they looked for a better slot machine or a more cooperative blackjack dealer.

Alex finally looked at Thorn again. She smothered a yawn in her fist, which seemed to trigger the same reaction in him. He laughed. "Does it seem to you that we've spent the last several days hungry or tired or both?" he asked.

"That's because we have."

"Well, now all we have to do is find out which hotel they're staying at and then we can finally get a good night's sleep."

Alex gestured at the glitzy casinos/hotels that rose about them like a neon forest. "There must be dozens of them."

He nodded wearily. "Well, they'd only go to the fancy ones, so that should limit our choices. All we have to do is think of a way to find the hotel before we drop dead on our feet, and then think of a way to find out which room they're staying in."

"You don't have any ideas?"

"Just one—we plaster her photo on every telephone pole in the city, like people do when their dog or cat runs away. Under it, in big letters, we'll write something along the lines of Missing: One Bride."

She smiled slowly. "And will you offer a reward for her return?"

He stared at her a second, then shook his head. "I honestly don't know, Alexandra." He paused and sighed. "Well, obviously I haven't the slightest idea where to start. How about you?"

"Actually, I do have an idea. I was thinking about this as we drove," she said. "What if we buy a dozen really splendid flower arrangements and have them delivered to the twelve most likely hotels. The one that accepts it has Natalie."

"Assuming she is still Jasmine Blackwell."

"We have to assume that or we'll go nuts."

"Have you ever wondered if she really is Jasmine Blackwell who pretended to be Natalie Dupree or Natalie Dupree pretending to be Jasmine Blackwell? I mean, maybe she's married to this Gerald character or maybe they're divorced. From the message on her machine, it's obvious she knew him long before she met me."

"Maybe this or that. Wait until you talk to her."

"You know, I'd about decided I was after revenge pure and simple, but now I think I've come full circle, that I just want to know what happened so that I can put this whole miserable experience behind me."

So you can put me behind you, too? Alex wondered, and the power of the encounter the night before filled her with sudden longing.

"I just want an end to it all. And after all this chasing and all these near misses, I need to wrap it up soon. Don't you feel that way, too, Alexandra? Because this started out as my problem, but good grief, you've been stuck in the middle of it with me so long, you have to have some kind of feelings about it."

What did he want her to say? The truth, that she resented his fixation because she'd been foolish enough to fall in love with him? She wasn't about to stretch herself out on that precarious limb so she repeated what she'd said the day before. "Remember the burning building? That's how I feel. Morbid curiosity, or maybe more to the point, this whole thing is like a book and I want to read the ending."

He studied his hands for a second before turning worried eyes to her. "Alexandra, about last night—"

"No, don't," she said, hoping he'd just let it drop.

"I got carried away," he said.

"We were both tired," she added.

"Fatigue can make you do crazy things."

Like act on your true emotions? she wondered.

He touched her arm. "I don't normally take a first kiss quite that far—"

"But it wasn't our first kiss," she said.

"You're referring to the train station?"

"No," she protested. "The other one."

Her statement was met with raised eyebrows. "What do you mean?"

He didn't know what she was talking about! For a second, her mind raced in circles trying to figure out how to avoid a subject she'd brought up, but then she thought, *Well, what the hell, what do I have to lose?* She said, "You kissed me at my sister's house. Don't look so confused. I believe you were asleep at the time. I think you had a dream about Natalie."

"And I grabbed you?" he asked, his face horrified.

"Yes."

He sighed deeply. "Alexandra, I'm sorry. I don't have any memory of it—"

"It's okay."

"Why didn't you slap **me**?"

She bit at her lip. Good question. Surely, after last night and the way she'd responded to him, he knew the answer. She shrugged and said, "Let's talk about the flowers."

For a couple of seconds he stared at her. "If that's the way you want it—"

"That's the way I want it. Okay, flowers at the hotels—"

"I don't see how we could cover the desks of twelve hotels. I don't think we have it in us to stake out that many establishments."

"Good point."

They were silent as they thought. At least, Alex tried to think, but her brain processes felt as though they were mired in tapioca pudding.

"Wait," he said at last. "What if we buy just one arrangement and then I deliver it to the hotels, starting with the most likely one first. When we finally find the right one, I'll take it up to the room and presto, ta dum!''

Alex wasn't sure if his idea was good or dumb because the tapioca pudding was beginning to congeal and she just couldn't think. She longed for a cold drink and a long bath and a soft bed. "Let's try it," she said.

First they had to find a florist, which took longer than it should have. It wasn't until they walked through the door of an air-conditioned shop that resembled the store Alex worked in that it occurred to her that most of the nicer hotels would have florists of their own and they needn't have run around town for thirty minutes looking for this one.

"What do we get?" Thorn asked as he stared at the cooler.

Alex, for the first time in many days, felt as though she'd come home. She gazed lovingly at buckets of roses in a multitude of colors, delphiniums, tall and graceful, snapdragons, poppies, anemones, carnations, freesia, lilies, tulips and all the rest. They were all perfect, nature's little treasures, all fresh and clean and so very beautiful.

"What's that dusky blue flower?" Thorn asked.

"Delphinium. Is that what you want?"

He stared into her eyes for the longest time, then he smiled slowly and shook his head. "Absolutely not. How about roses. Seems to me all women like roses."

"What's not to like?"

He frowned. "Hell, what do I care if she likes the flowers? I'll probably throw them at her."

"Temper, temper," she teased.

"Let's get something cheap and ugly."

Alex turned to the woman who had come forward to help them. "A dozen pink carnations," she said.

"Those are too pretty," he grumbled as the woman plucked a dozen stems from the vase in the cooler.

"Yeah, well they're all too pretty," she quipped. "Besides, I get to hold them while you drive, and these smell wonderful.''

They watched intently as the woman wrapped the flowers and a few branches of fern in clear plastic. She tied the bundle with a rose-colored ribbon, and Thorn paid for them with a credit card.

They started with the closest hotel, which was fancy enough, but Thorn was met at the desk by a blank stare when he asked for Jasmine Blackwell. Two more tries produced the same results. The fourth hotel was brand-new.

It was called the Golden Hind after the ship Sir Francis Drake had used to complete the first circumnavigation of the world undertaken by an Englishman in 1577. This information was carved into a plaque by the front doors. A gold plaque, of course.

The interior of the hotel/casino also relied heavily on gold to make its point. Gold counters, gold wallpaper, gold fixtures, gold uniforms; everywhere Thorn and Alex looked they found gold. And hanging from the high ceiling in the lobby, looking like a twenty-four-karat ghost ship, was a golden replica of the old sailing vessel.

"I'd bet you a bar of solid gold that they're here," Thorn whispered into Alex's ear.

She nodded as she separated from him and stood off to the side where she could still hear what he said. Thorn approached the counter and launched into his story.

"I have flowers for—" he consulted a card Alex had tucked in with the flowers "—a Jasmine Blackwell."

The desk clerk consulted his computer. Alex knew they had hit pay dirt when he said, "You can leave them with us, sir."

"Can't do it. I have orders to deliver a message with the flowers. A personal message."

The clerk shook his head. "Write it down or tell it to me. We don't give out room numbers to *anyone*."

Thorn paused only momentarily before handing over the flowers.

The clerk turned bored eyes to Thorn as he set the flowers on the counter. "Well," he said at last, "what's the message?"

Now Thorn looked trapped as well as irritated, and Alex smiled into her hand. "Uh, the sparrow flies at midnight," he finally blurted out.

The clerk looked up from the flowers. With a sneer, he barked, "What kind of message is that?"

"Hell, I don't know," Thorn growled. "Maybe she's a spy."

"Are you some kind of wise guy—"

Thorn clenched his fists. "Listen, buddy—"

Alex grabbed his arm. "Come on, Henry," she said, glancing at the clerk. "You're late for your medication."

The desk clerk, somewhat appeased, sniffed. She pulled Thorn toward the door. Regathering his composure, Thorn shook her free. "I can't leave here."

"We'll go out this door and in another one. The clerk is watching." She looked up at him and added, "'The sparrow flies at midnight'?"

He held the door for her and they quickly walked down the sidewalk. "Yeah? Well, how about your line to the waitress at the Space Needle?"

They reentered the building and made their way toward the counter. Alex could still see the pink flowers on the desk. "What line?"

"I quote. 'She killed our parents.'"

"Oh, that. Well, I guess neither one of us are fast thinkers."

A bellboy appeared. Alex and Thorn watched as the clerk gave him the flowers. The boy got in the elevator; miraculously, no one else did.

"Remember which floor lights up," Thorn whispered.

They both watched as the elevator rose to the twelfth floor and stopped.

"That does it. They're on the twelfth floor."

Probably, Alex thought. Maybe not, though. Maybe he had another delivery to make, maybe he stopped to let someone else on. Who knew? The Shadow did? Jeez, she was getting rummy.

Thorn marched across the lobby and approached a different person at the desk. Alex followed.

"I need a room, preferably on the twelfth floor," she heard him say.

"What are you doing?" she whispered.

"Getting us a room. You look beat and I feel like an old shoe. Might as well get a room close to you know who."

She started to protest, but the unmistakable fact of the matter was that he was right. "Get two rooms," she said.

"Two?"

"We don't need to be joined at the hip any longer, Thorn." *And I've got to look out for my heart,* she added internally.

"Oh. Well, I suppose you're right," he said, but he looked perplexed and perhaps even a little abandoned.

You're here because of Natalie, not because of me, she tried to tell him with her eyes, so that he would understand the rejection came not from her, but actually, from him. However, the puzzled look remained and she steeled her heart against it.

Luggage retrieved from the car, they rode the elevator up to the twelfth floor. Gaudy gold doors greeted them, doors that were side by side.

He stared at her. "Which one do you want?"

"I don't know—" Her words were cut short by the appearance of a man with a long white ponytail. He got off the elevator and walked past them as they both held their breath and tried to be invisible. Gerald Blackwell nodded politely at them before using a key to enter a room across the hall from theirs. A brief glimpse into the suddenly bright interior revealed a blaze of pink—the carnations—sitting on a desk, then Blackwell closed the door behind him and they were alone again.

Thorn softly whistled. "How about that for timing!"

"Incredible," Alex agreed. "The whole thing has just been dropped right into your lap."

"I wonder where *she* is."

"How do you know she's not in the room?"

"Because he had to switch on the lights. You know, Alexandra, that man looks familiar. I didn't see his face clearly in the Space Needle but I could swear I've seen him somewhere before."

"Maybe he visited Natalie in Cottage Grove—"

"No, that's not it. Well, it will come to me."

"Anyway, maybe Natalie is in that room taking a nap—"

"Not Natalie, not in the middle of the day. I bet you she's shopping."

"Well, go knock and find out," Alex said.

"I can't."

She stared at him with incredulous eyes. "Why not?"

"Because what in the world do I say if she's not in there?"

"Good grief, Thorn! We've come all this way. I would think you'd demand to know where she is and then go find her. Why are you hesitating?"

"Because I don't want to talk to Gerald Blackwell without Natalie around. Truth of the matter is, I don't even want to talk to *her* right this second."

Alex leaned against the wall and shook her head. "I don't get it."

He lifted her chin with his finger. "Look at me," he said softly. "I've got big black sacks beneath my eyes, my clothes look like I've slept in them because, hey, I've slept in them, and I'm grimy and grumpy. If Natalie sees me like this, she'll know how much she hurt me. I don't want to give her the satisfaction. I have an idea for a way to go about this that lets me cover myself. All I have to do is check out a few things, maybe bribe a busboy or a desk clerk—''

"Do you always go around bribing people?"

"Just recently."

She sighed. "Okay, we'll do it your way. What do you want me to do?"

"Nothing," he said, and smiling mysteriously, opened the first door, handed the key to Alex and gently pushed her over the threshold. "Get some sleep," he added. "We have a big night ahead of us."

"But—"

"No buts. Go to sleep."

And then he closed the door and Alex was left in her golden room all by herself, alone for the first time since the police station. "Get used to it, kiddo," she told herself before flinging her weary body down on the gold bedspread. For one second, she wondered what he was up to, but curiosity was quickly killed by a wave of fatigue that washed her into a deep sleep.

Thorn returned to his room within thirty minutes. He walked with assurance born of the knowledge that he could not possibly meet Natalie in the hallway because she was downstairs in the catacombs of the hotel shops getting a facial. Thanks to a couple of agreeable employees, his wallet was a good deal lighter, but he was wealthy in information.

With effort, he passed Alexandra's door, fighting the urge to knock and tell her what he'd arranged. On second thought, he went into his room and wrote a short note on a piece of hotel stationery, which he was amused if not surprised to see was ivory paper embossed with a gold ship, and slipped it beneath her door where she'd find it when she awoke.

He put in a call to the desk to be buzzed at 6:00 p.m., took a small white box from his pocket and set it by the phone, then settled onto his own bed with a groan of contentment. With the shades drawn it could be one-thirty in the morning instead of one-thirty in the afternoon. No reason not to drift off to a soul-satisfying sleep. The night was ahead, the cleaners had his tux, retribution for Natalie was planned; everything was as right with the world as could be.

Laying in the dark, he found he missed the soft sound of Alexandra's breathing beside him. He'd grown accustomed to her being there, to talking to her before drifting off to sleep. Like a flash, the night before flooded his brain and he temporarily relived the feel of her skin, of her lips, of her wonderful curves and her smoldering warmth.

How he had wanted to make love to her! In retrospect, it was probably wise that she pulled back; after all, he was looking for one woman who had broken his heart. No need to complicate his life with another woman. Anyway, he'd trusted a woman once before and look what had happened.

But Alexandra isn't like that.

This renegade thought was like an ice pick in the brain but the truth of it settled over him like a cozy blanket. Alexandra wasn't like that. And it wasn't a guess, either. He knew her. He knew she wouldn't lie and cheat. He knew her.

Well, she's your friend.

This thought was another stab with the pick because it was true and yet it wasn't. Sure, she was his friend in that he cared about her and she seemed to care about him. He liked her. She was fun and unexpected and trustworthy and she couldn't drink worth a damn. She left keys in the lock, she said outrageous things, she was soft and tender and sweet. Another vivid flash, this time of Alexandra holding her sister's baby, touching the child's pink cheek, care and love flooding her eyes.

His friend. But friends don't almost make love.

And you wanted her.

Desperately.

He sat up, stood and laid back down. He tried to recall the night in Tacoma and the kiss she said they'd shared. She hadn't flattened his nose about it or even woken him to protest, which meant that she'd enjoyed it. Didn't it? Surely her politeness didn't extend to accepting unwanted advances! Wait, what in the hell was going on? *When had this little mission stopped being about Natalie Dupree and started being about Alexandra Williams!*

He rolled over on his side and pushed all thoughts of Alexandra from his mind. He finally fell asleep by thinking about fields of those stalks of flowers he'd seen at the florist shop, the dusky blue ones. Delphiniums, that's what she'd said they were called. Delphiniums.

Alex awoke abruptly, flinging out her arm to touch Thorn. Her hand met an empty bed and she sat up, groggy and a little disoriented. Where she was and why she was there came flooding back, and she glanced at the digital clock on the table beside her bed. It flashed 5:02. She wasn't sure which 5:02 it was, a.m. or p.m., so she crossed to the shades and drew them open. It was bright outside.

After a long shower, which washed some of the cobwebs out of her brain, she wrapped herself in a big towel and turned on the light near the closet. That was when she found a piece of folded paper in front of the door.

"Dinner tonight at seven o'clock," it read. "Hope your sister sent along a pretty dress. Guess who we'll be seated by?"

She smiled. Guess, indeed. She put the paper aside and opened her suitcase, taking out the peach-colored cotton dress she'd borrowed from Vicky. There were a few wrinkles in the cloth, but maybe she could steam them out with the shower. She hung it over the door and stared at it for almost five minutes before digging through her purse to see how much of Vicky's money she had left. Quite a bit. Of course, the money would have to be repaid once she got home and regained access to her checking account. Biting her lips she made a hasty decision, and threw the peach dress back in the bag. What was the point of life if you didn't splurge once in a while? She quickly put on the jean shorts and a T-shirt, combed her hair and, grabbing her purse, carefully opened the door.

The hall was clear. She *really* didn't want to bump into Natalie. Knowing Natalie would never use them, she opted for the stairs.

As she suspected, while the first three floors of the hotel were devoted to gambling and restaurants, and the top fifteen stories to rooms, the basement was crowded with shops. She found a dress shop and, looking inside cautiously, assured herself Natalie was nowhere in sight.

A woman with short white hair approached her at once. "May I help you?"

"I need a dress for tonight," Alex told her. "A special dress. I have very little time and only two hundred and twenty-eight dollars to my name. That sounds like a lot of money to me, but I imagine in a place like this, it isn't, so I guess I'm hoping you might have a sale rack or...something."

The woman narrowed her eyes and gave Alex a professional once-over. "Size 6?"

"Or an 8. But I'm short—"

"A petite. Well, you're right. That's not a lot of money in a place like this. But we do have a rental program here. Eighty-eight dollars for one night. The selection isn't great, but there's a gold lamé dress that we just got in, never been worn, and it's gorgeous. I believe it will fit you perfectly."

Gold lamé? Well, what other color would be in this

place! Alex took out her money. "Eighty-eight dollars just to *rent* a dress?"

"Outrageous, isn't it?"

She reviewed her choices, which took all of five seconds. "Okay."

"I don't think you'll be disappointed."

With the dress hidden away in a garment bag, Alex retraced her steps toward the stairs. She passed a men's store and something in the window caught her eye. Something wonderful, something she knew she had to buy. Inside, she found she could just afford it. Maybe she'd only have five dollars left to her name, but what the heck!

The next shop on the way was a beauty shop and she thought longingly of someone fixing her hair, but as she was now almost broke, knew she had to be satisfied with peering through the glass walls. And that's when she saw Natalie, sitting in a beautician's chair, her hair in the last stages of a comb-out, her eyes idle.

Alex immediately turned her back to the glass and prayed that Natalie hadn't seen *her*. As she hurried away, she wondered if she should tell Thorn what had happened. The only good thing about it, she decided as she entered the elevator, was that placing Natalie had obliterated the need to climb twelve flights of stairs. Nap or no nap, her body still felt heavy with fatigue, her joints ached and the beginning of a headache throbbed in her temples.

Thorn grabbed the phone on the first ring and listened as a mechanical voice told him to get his buns out of bed, or words to that effect. He found his tux had been pressed and returned to his room, and before he showered, he ran a damp cloth over his black shoes.

By six forty-five, he had butterflies in his stomach, as though he was preparing for a performance on a stage, a debut performance. He was a simple man, used to other guys and cows and football games. Did Alexandra like football?

Stop thinking about her! he demanded of himself.

What he wasn't used to were scenes. He had no intention of making one tonight; all he envisioned was a conversation between adults, a few choice words said, a few loose ends tied neatly in knots, Natalie a thing of the past, history. And Alexandra?

Yes, his heart said. Damn the torpedoes, the truth of the matter was that this fiasco had yielded a bonus; it had thrown him and Alexandra Williams together, where he hoped they would spend the rest of their lives. He tried not to think about the fact that she'd called off the lovemaking the night before or that she'd called him shallow and said that they weren't anything alike. That was garbage, they were just alike.

Pep talk given, he fixed his bow tie and checked himself out in the mirror. The image he saw almost completely resembled the one he'd last seen the morning of his wedding day. The same clothes, the same slicked-back hair. Not the same expression, however. Not the dreamy-eyed man who was marrying, whom he believed to be, the most fascinating woman in the world. This man looked older, more experienced in the ways of love, more sure of what love really was and wasn't.

For the first time since he'd begun this headlong chase to confront Natalie, he found his resolve wavering. The small white box beside the phone caught his eye and he picked it up, turning it over and over in his hands, smiling when he thought about what lay within. Alexandra—she was the trouble. His thoughts kept circling back to her, which lessened his need to face the woman who had abandoned him.

No, he thought firmly. *You've come this far, go on and finish the job.* Besides, he reminded himself. There was another necklace to consider, one he wouldn't want to see around Alexandra's neck, not after it had rested on Natalie. But he'd have children someday or maybe his sister should have it—at any rate, he couldn't walk away from it.

Before he could fall prey to any more internal dialogue, he pocketed the white box and left the room.

He knocked on Alexandra's door and waited impatiently for her to answer. He'd called her room right after he woke and he'd found her out of breath but awake. "I've been downstairs," she told him. "I'll be ready on time, don't worry."

Now she called out his name and told him to come in. He let himself in the room, closing the door behind him.

"You should really keep this door locked—" he began, but by then he had turned to see her and words failed him.

Her hair was loose around her face, enchanting wisps of stray dark curls touching her cheeks and forehead. Her deep blue eyes were dramatically made up, all traces of the black eye gone, her lips ruby red like hot cinnamon candy. Beautiful white shoulders were bare.

The dress was gold lamé and it took his breath away. It wrapped her breasts and torso with the sinewy grasp of a lover, hugged her hips, flared around her legs. A slit on the left side gave tantalizing glimpses of a shapely leg and he smiled when he recognized the gold sandals with the flowers on the toe.

"Do I look okay?" she asked. She glanced down at her feet and added, "They were the only shoes I had that matched."

He finally found his voice. "You look wonderful. Way, way too nice to have to ask a man for a compliment. I apologize, but honestly, Alexandra, you knocked the wind out of me. I can't believe Vicky loaned you that dress and it was stuffed in that little duffel bag all this time—"

"Hardly."

"Then where did you get it?"

She smiled mysteriously. "Don't you worry about that."

He continued staring at her. Once before he'd been struck by how much a stranger this woman could seem, and yet in the next breath she'd turned back into herself. She'd done this for him. Or had she? Maybe she'd done it for herself or even for Natalie.

"You look very nice, too," she said. "Very, very dashing."

"Thanks. Oh, I almost forgot," he added as he reached into his pocket. "I have something for you." He opened the small white box and withdrew a delicate gold charm hanging from a fine gold chain.

"I thought of you the minute I saw this," he said as he fastened it around her neck. He turned her slightly so she could see herself in the mirror.

"Oh, Thorn," she gasped.

He felt like gasping too as he stared at her reflection in the mirror; a delicate gold rendition of a chocolate kiss, complete with three small diamonds, rested on her bosom just above her cleavage, sparkling there like a tiny star, making him think of hidden treats and the night before when they'd briefly been his to savor.

"Sweets for the sweet," he said, and his voice was husky.

She bit at her lip. "You shouldn't have. It's lovely, just lovely."

He caught her shoulders. Her skin was so soft, it almost melted beneath his hands. "I wanted to thank you, Alexandra. I wanted to give you something you'd have always, that would remind you of this time we've had together."

She nodded, but the joy on her face seemed to be replaced by sadness. Why was that? For a long second she stared at him, then finally she seemed to shrug off whatever thought had made her look unhappy. "I have something for you, too," she said, and turning toward the bed, took the lid from a large box.

She presented him with a black hat, a cowboy hat.

"I hope it fits," she said.

A smile twisted his stomach. She'd bought him a Stetson. He swallowed painfully around the lump that suddenly appeared in his throat. Horrified, he realized his eyes stung with tears.

"You don't like it," she said.

He took the hat from her hands. "Like it? It's the best gift anyone has ever given me. I love it." He pulled it on over his head and looked down at her. "Well?"

"It fits you like a glove. Of course, I imagine you'll like it better after a good stampede or a heavy downpour."

"Not this beauty, not on your life." He ran two fingers along the brim and added, "I needed a new hat. Thanks, Alexandra." He leaned down to kiss her and she turned a cheek toward his lips. Not exactly what he'd had in mind!

"You don't have to wear it tonight," she told him. "I realize it might not be appropriate."

"It's damn appropriate!" he erupted, and then before he could stop himself, explained. "I wanted to wear a hat on my wedding day. It's who I am. Truth of the matter is, I feel half-naked without a hat. Natalie was horrified when I told her about it. She said it would ruin the wedding. Ha! That's a laugh, isn't it? *Me* spoil the wedding!"

"Natalie, Natalie," Alexandra said softly, and *the* look was back on her face. He had the sudden feeling he shouldn't have mentioned Natalie's name.

"Why did I let her influence me like that?" he continued. It was as if there were an open faucet in his voice box.

Alexandra looked down at the floor.

"I know you think it was sex, sex, sex, and I admit, that played a large role in my attraction to her. But I was ready to walk down the aisle with a woman I barely knew, a woman who didn't like anything about my life, a woman who apparently didn't even like me! What in the world was I thinking?"

"Maybe you weren't thinking," she said swiftly.

He lifted her chin. "Maybe I wasn't. Maybe I should get down on my knees and thank Natalie or Jasmine or whatever the hell her name is."

Alex smiled. "Is that your new plan?"

His former doubts had vanished. "Not on your life. Tonight she gets what she has coming to her. I'm not letting her off the hook. No way."

"Then we'd better go," Alexandra said, turning to the mirror. He watched her dab around her eyes with a tissue, fixing her makeup, he guessed. She looked beautiful and yet he was suddenly shot with the irrational desire to see her in the ocean or on a horse or in the bright sweatshirt she'd worn for days with the self-assurance of a princess. Damn, he even missed the parachute pants.

Look at her, he thought as he watched her put a few items away and check herself over, her gaze carefully avoiding his. A beautiful woman in an incredible dress, perfect hair and skin, perfect makeup. Where was the Alexandra he'd come to know? Who was this lovely creature, this stranger?

And it wasn't just the way she looked, either. He had the feeling she was biting back her words, that her thoughts were running ahead like the wind, leaving him in the dust. For days he'd felt as though she was a sister; well, okay, not a sister, but at least someone who was open and understandable. Now he wasn't sure. Now she seemed remote and withdrawn and very mysterious. What was going on here!

Alex noticed that Thorn chose the elevator with the confidence of a man who *knows* the person he doesn't want to meet won't be met. "They have reservations for seventhirty," he whispered in her ear. "Knowing Natalie, that means we can expect them about eight o'clock."

Alex nodded. For a second back in her room, he'd seen

her as a woman, a desirable woman; she'd sensed it, and in that instant she'd woven a future for them beyond tonight, beyond Natalie.

But she was kidding herself—that had become apparent as he rambled on and on. And now, as he threw details at her—the restaurant, the adjoining tables in a private corner—she thought ahead to the end of the evening, then further ahead to the long ride home and the dismal prospect of the days and weeks to follow where she wouldn't see him. Her head began to ache again.

She found her hand had risen to clasp the small gold chocolate kiss he'd placed around her neck. Even the words he'd used when he gave it to her foreshadowed the inevitability of an end to their relationship. He'd said something like, "This is so you'll remember our time together." Those words implied there would be no further time spent together.

She dropped her hand and looked up at him. He winked conspiratorially at her. Brother, but did he look wonderful in that hat, the dark brim shadowing his gray eyes, suggesting secrets any woman would kill herself to discover. She dropped her gaze. Why had she allowed herself to fall in love with this guy? She felt dizzy with frustration.

At last the elevator came to a stop. They waited until everyone else left, then Thorn took her arm. His grasp was firm on her bare skin, and she was flooded with memories of other times he'd held her, other times his touch had inflamed her with desire.

They passed crowded gaming tables and rows of slot machines, then stepped onto an escalator that rose two flights to a restaurant accessible in only that manner. Thorn stopped at the entrance and pulled her aside. He stared at her, as though searching for words.

"What is it?" she prompted.

Still he stared at her, but then slowly, the corners of his mouth turned up. "I don't need to do this," he said.

She had no idea what he was talking about. "Don't need to do what?"

"This. I don't need to see Natalie. I thought about forgetting this whole thing earlier, but I convinced myself it had to be done. Now that I'm here, with you...well, perhaps there's a better way to retrieve...things. I just don't feel the need to confront her and possibly embarrass you—"

"Oh, no, you don't," Alex interrupted.

"Alexandra—"

She shook her head vehemently. "We have not traveled for six days through three states for you to back out now. You're going to face this damn woman and close this chapter of your life or I'm going to scream!"

"Why are you so adamant about this?"

Because I love you. Because I want you for my own, but not with Natalie hovering in the back of your mind, hovering in the back of our lives. She said, "I just am. Now, let's go."

He stared at her again, and finally he nodded. "Maybe you're right."

"I'm right."

He chuckled "Okay, but when this is all over, we need to talk."

She looked up at him and came within an inch of touching his lips. "What about?"

"Us," he said.

"There is no us—"

"Like hell there isn't," he interrupted. Then he grinned at her. "Right now, you're absolutely right, we're finally on the verge of wrapping up this little chase. Natalie is about to have the shock of her life. Your burning building is about to topple to the ground, Miss Williams, and you're going to have a front-row seat."

Alex nodded, but the thought resurfaced, the thought that Thorn was still infatuated with Natalie, perhaps even in love with her. He'd protest it, she knew that, but she could tell by the tone of his voice, by the lifting of his spirits just knowing Natalie was coming. Maybe someday he'd get over the woman, but right now he was charged with excitement and it was because of Natalie.

He was still in love with her. Alex fought the desire to run away.

Chapter Ten

The restaurant was called the Treasure Trove, and elaborate chests of gold bullion and brilliant jewels lay scattered about between tables while the waitresses wore eye patches, white halter tops and short gold skirts that just barely covered their derrieres. Alex assumed the treasures were phony, but they sure glittered and sparkled like the real thing! *And I fit right in,* she acknowledged with a glance at her dress. She wasn't sure how she felt about this.

The walls were adorned with gilded nautical artifacts; gas torches created wavering light, which made the atmosphere appear wild and wicked. As the burnt sienna ceiling was nubby in texture and the dividing walls were thick with rounded corners, she supposed one was expected to feel as though they were in a fairly luxurious cave inhabited by scantily clad women.

"What do you think?" Thorn asked her as they followed one of the latter to a table.

"I think it's a little over the top. What about you?"

"Not exactly my taste. It's brand-new and expensive,

though, so I knew Natalie would make reservations here, and I was right.''

Their table was one of two set in a small nook. The other table was empty. Thorn seated Alex, then took off his hat and handed it to the waitress. "Take good care of this," he told her, and added, "as well as the other details we discussed this afternoon. Remember who to seat here and remember to disappear for a while." Alex saw him slip her money before he seated himself.

"More bribes?" she said.

"More bribes. Should be the last one, however. Well, would you like something to drink while we wait?"

Alex nodded. "Nothing alcoholic," she murmured. She felt nervous about the upcoming showdown and also silly for having spent so much money to doll herself up. Why had she done that, what was the point?

You did it for him, you ninny. You silly fool.

For him. So she'd look like Natalie? What a joke!

"So?" he said.

She'd been lost in the quagmire of her thoughts. "I beg your pardon?"

Leaning forward, his hands covering hers, he said, "I asked you what you were thinking about."

"Nothing," she said as she withdrew her hands.

He folded his now-empty hands together and leveled a foggy stare at her. "I don't buy it. As a matter of fact, you seem different tonight. Kind of quiet and introspective."

He stopped grilling her as the waitress set two tall glasses in front of them. "Ice tea," he said as she left.

Alexandra took a grateful sip. "Thanks."

"You are most welcome. Alexandra, you really look wonderful in that dress. I can't imagine where you found it or how you paid for it, but it's stunning on you."

She thanked him again.

"Um, I was wondering. Where are the parachute pants?"

His question startled her. "The red ones?"

"Yeah. And the sweatshirt with the funny sleeves. I liked that sweatshirt."

"Well, so did I. Did I ever thank you for buying me those clothes? I should have. Anyway, my sister kept them."

Incredibly, he looked disappointed. "Oh."

"They were kind of dirty, Thorn. She'll wash them and send them back to me."

He nodded.

The waitress appeared again with menus. Thorn opened his, but Alex left hers folded on the table.

"Aren't you hungry?"

"I guess I'm too nervous," she admitted.

"But you have to eat—"

"Maybe later." She was suddenly wishing she'd agreed with him when he wanted to forgo this event, and that they were on their way back to her room for the talk he seemed determined to have with her. However, while she was now filled with trepidation, Thorn seemed revitalized and totally focused, back on track, damn the torpedoes. They were seesawing back and forth.

"I'm getting sick to my stomach," she mumbled.

She noticed that he suddenly raised the menu to hide his face. Looking at her around the side of it he said, "Don't get sick now, honey. Guess who just showed up."

She didn't have to guess. The look of anticipation on Thorn's face and the excited tone of his voice told her exactly who had just entered. And then she was aware of the rustle of satin beside her and a flash of royal blue as Natalie passed and was seated in a chair, her back to Thorn's back.

They waited while drink orders were given. Thorn lowered his menu and took a quick peek over his shoulder. Alex watched his smile fade as he studied Natalie's back, the ivory skin, the tendrils of reddish hair that escaped her elaborate hairdo, the glitter of diamonds and sapphires around her neck.

Was he recalling the feel of her skin, the glistening shine of her hair as it fell onto his face when she leaned over him? Alex felt faint with these images.

He reached over and touched Natalie's shoulder.

As Natalie turned, Alex steeled herself for whatever happened next. She was glad they were semisecluded so that Thorn's angry voice wouldn't thunder throughout the restaurant. She snuck a peek at Gerald Blackwell's distinctive face and felt a stab of pity for the man who was bound to be caught up in the impending scene.

"Why, Natalie," Thorn said to Natalie's horrified expression. "I thought it was you! Just imagine finding you here." He glanced back at Alex. "Look, Alexandra, it's your good friend, Natalie Dupree."

Surprised and pleased by Thorn's low-key approach, Alex had no trouble producing a smile. Natalie's look was priceless. The woman was fair-skinned anyway, but Alex could have sworn she lost even more color as she faced Thorn, seemingly speechless, eyes round with shock.

"Friends of yours, my dear?" Gerald Blackwell said. His eyes registered faint recognition. He was obviously trying to remember where he'd first seen Thorn and Alex

"We're across the hall from you," Alex said helpfully. "Of course, we had no idea you were with Natalie."

Natalie finally found her voice. "Thorn?" It was more of a squeak.

"Yes, Nat, it's me. Amazing, huh?" He turned his attention to Blackwell. "Let me introduce myself. I'm Thorn Powell, the man your lovely dinner companion was supposed to marry last Saturday. But you gave her a whistle and she scampered off to meet you instead. Oh, I assume it was you and not someone else?" He looked back at Natalie. "Gee, have I been indiscreet?"

"What are you doing here? And with *her!*"

Alex smiled at Natalie, who refused to meet her eyes. Over the past few days, seen at first through Thorn's heartbroken eyes and then with growing betrayal, Natalie had assumed larger-than-life status. And now, here she was, a flesh-and-blood woman with nice skin and good taste in clothes—and men. A co-worker with no love of her job, a woman who hadn't made it on her own, who had hooked on to a man—any man as long as he was upwardly mobile—to make it for her.

Thorn turned his attention back to Blackwell. "Where are my manners? This beautiful young woman with me is Alexandra Williams. She was Natalie's friend, and oh, I almost forgot, her maid of honor, too."

Alexandra smiled brightly. "Hello," she said, as though she was an innocent bystander at some bizarre dinner party.

"Are you expecting me to believe that you and Alex just happened to show up here?" This, from Natalie.

Thorn looked perplexed. "Now how else would we have chanced to run into you like this?"

"I don't know. You must have followed us or something."

Thorn laughed. "Hardly. Alexandra and I just hopped in the car for a mad spree in Reno. What, you think we purposely followed you to the Golden Hind because we missed you so much? Is that it?"

Gerald cleared his throat. "Natalie, they couldn't have followed us. Be reasonable. You know as well as I do how many places we've been the last few days and how many modes of transportation we've employed." He looked at Thorn and added, "Listen, old man, I owe you an apology—"

"Don't you apologize to him!" Natalie again. Loud, too.

"Lower your voice," Gerald snapped. Alex was amused to see that Natalie obeyed him. Boy, this guy must *really* be loaded if with a mere snarl, he could get her to toe the line.

"I just mean that you have nothing to apologize to him about, sweetie," she crooned. "He's a fool, a nobody."

"That's true," Thorn said, shaking his head dramatically. "I am a fool. Just a silly rancher who made a major mistake about a woman. There are lots of us around, you know. You might want to be careful, you may be a silly fool, too."

"Don't listen to him, Conrad."

"Conrad?" Thorn said, narrowing his eyes and casting Gerald Blackwell a longer, more intense stare.

"Gerald," Natalie said quickly with a sidelong look at Blackwell. "I meant *Gerald*."

Thorn suddenly erupted into laughter. "By God, that's it! You're not Gerald Blackwell, you're Conrad Tibourn of Tibourn Oil. Good grief, no wonder she dumped me faster than a steer dumps a cowboy at a rodeo!" He looked back at Alex and added, "I told you I'd seen him somewhere. His picture is in the paper all the time. He's something like the third wealthiest man in the country. And, if I'm not mistaken, a married man at that!"

"Please," Conrad said, his voice hushed.

"He's leaving his wife," Natalie said with confidence. Or maybe not. Maybe what Alexandra heard in Natalie's voice was bravado, not confidence.

Conrad Tibourn looked around him as though he was afraid spies had suddenly sprouted from the fake treasure chests. "Natalie, keep your voice down!" he hissed.

Alex looked at the man's hands. Sure enough, a slender gold band encircled the ring finger of his left hand. She glanced at Natalie's hands and found Thorn's diamond, the huge monster Natalie had waxed poetic about since the day he slipped it on her finger. A huge, emerald-shaped diamond flanked with sapphires.

Thorn said, "Let me guess. You've known Conrad for a long time, right, Natalie? A little hanky-panky, hmm, Conrad?"

"See here—"

"But there's that pesky wife. Does she own controlling interest in your company, Tibourn? Is that why you can't leave her—"

"He *is* leaving her," Natalie said.

Thorn shook his head. "If he was leaving her, why is he using a phony name with you? Face it, baby, you're being conned."

Conrad Tibourn stood abruptly. "Natalie, I think we'd better leave."

"Not on our account, I hope," Thorn said. He touched Natalie's hand and added, "Oh, by the way, thanks for the parking tickets." Looking back at Tibourn, he added, "You might want to be careful about loaning her your car."

Natalie frowned at him. It was obvious to Alex that Natalie had bigger problems right that second than Thorn's sarcasm. Conrad Tibourn, for instance, who looked about ready to implode.

Natalie, standing, took Conrad's arm. "Sweetie?"

Conrad turned his black eyes onto Natalie, who visibly shrank under their scrutiny. "We're leaving," he said.

Thorn stood, too. "I think you have something of mine," he said, and in his voice was a tone Alex had never before heard.

Natalie twisted at the diamond on her finger.

"No, not that. You can throw that thing down the drain for all I care. You know what I mean."

Her hand flew to her throat.

"That's right."

"You gave it to me," Natalie said.

"Yeah, well, I suppose we each gave the other something important. You gave me promises, I gave you a wedding present, a piece of heirloom jewelry. You took back your promises, now I plan to take back the necklace." He glanced down at Alex and added, "Maybe someday I'll be blessed with a daughter. If that happens, I want her to have her great-grandmother's jewels." Looking back at Natalie, he said, "It's simple, Natalie. You either take it off yourself, or I'll take it off for you."

Natalie began to protest. Tibourn swore. "Give him the blasted thing, Natalie. Let's go." And with that, he swept past her and walked away.

Natalie fumbled with the clasp. The necklace finally came free and she threw it down on the table. With one last furious glance at Alex, she was off after Tibourn.

Before Thorn sat back in his chair, he scooped up the necklace and dropped it into his pocket, then sighed heavily and grinned. "You were right, Alexandra, that did need to be done. I thought it went rather well. What about you?"

Alex was still reeling from the revelations and the wrath she'd just witnessed. Cradling her head in her hand, she stared at him. "I suppose…"

"I don't know about you, but I feel a lot better. Nothing like being dumped for a genuine millionaire to make a man feel like a man."

She pushed damp bangs away from her forehead as she leaned forward. Thorn's face temporarily blurred and she realized she'd been more upset by everything than she originally thought. "Was it worth it, Thorn? Was all the travel and the mixups and the jail and the fatigue worth confronting Natalie?"

"You were the one who insisted I do this—"

"Answer me."

He thought for a moment. "I suppose it's inevitable that things weren't quite as dramatic as I pictured them in the dead of night as I lay awake thinking of ways to kill her without getting caught. But, yes, I've tied up the loose ends. Natalie is Conrad Tibourn's problem now, and he's hers! You must feel the same way because you have a pretty rosy glow to your face. So, do you feel as though you've read the end of your book?"

"No," she said, but when he pressed her, she refused to

explain. The Natalie chapters had been interesting, but for Alex, only a filler for the real story, the story that had been building in her heart. She looked at Thorn and added, "I'm tired and I'm not really hungry. If you'll excuse me, I'll go up to bed. You stay and have dinner."

He stood as she did. "Don't leave. I wanted to talk to you about us—"

"I said before that there is no us."

"But last night in the car—"

"Was a mistake."

"You forget that I was there, too. It was no mistake." He caught her hands and drew her around the table, pulling her into his embrace.

"Thorn, don't," she said, protesting.

"Don't what?" he asked as he kissed her throat and added, "You're awfully, warm, Alexandra. Are you okay?"

She tried to push him away but both her wrists seemed to be broken and nothing happened. "This isn't about me," she mumbled. "It's about you. Whether you realize it or not, you're on the rebound at best, still in love with her at worst. You've been consumed by Natalie for so long that you need time to discover your true emotions."

"I have discovered my true emotions. That's what I'm trying to tell you."

"You rushed ahead before, and look where it landed you," she murmured. Her throat felt so dry.

"It landed me here, with you, though I admit it was a rather circuitous route."

"You don't know how you feel," she said.

"I know how I feel about you," he protested, staring down into her eyes. "Delphiniums," he added tenderly. "That's the color of your eyes. Dusky blue delphiniums."

She felt like fainting. Her heart raced, her limbs felt heavy.

"Alexandra, don't you understand? This whole chase

stopped being about Natalie days ago. I've been dragging you hither and yon because I wanted to be with *you!* It's you I love. Sure, I was infatuated with Natalie, but I never loved her, not the way I love you. You're like a part of me, honey, as important as my lungs or my heart. I want you to marry me—''

"No, no. Natalie—''

"Hush. You said you weren't beautiful or mysterious or manipulative, that you weren't my kind of woman. Hogwash! You're gorgeous, inside and out. You're as mysterious a woman as I ever want to be tangled up with, and you've manipulated my heart right into your pocket. Honey, we have so much in common, so much to explore. I want you to have Sprite. She's perfect for you. And then there's this stand of fir trees that will make you feel so good inside. And the stars, honey, think about all the stories you need to tell me about them. You have all the qualities I want in a woman who will be the mother of my children. You're honest and real and fun and bright and I've got so much to share with you. Don't you see? Land galore, land for you to have a cat—hell, ten cats! I'll build you a greenhouse for your flowers. And there's this pond—Alexandra?''

She smiled up at him. What a lovely fairy tale he told, full of kings and dragons and deep moats. No, no...his words were suddenly hollow, as though spoken from a great distance. As he stared at her, his mouth moving but no words coming out, she felt as though she was caught in a tornado, lifted from her feet, spun around and around, then deposited in a heap, beyond comprehension, lost in the all-encompassing dark.

Thorn sat in a chair by the door, jacket draped across the foot of the bed, tie off, sleeves rolled up, staring across the dimly lit room toward the woman he loved. Alexandra was asleep under his covers; the doctor was gone. For a second, he recalled the panic of her collapsing in his arms, the long ride in the elevator, him carrying her, refusing to let the hotel officials whisk her off to a hospital. The doctor had said she was exhausted and also that she'd become dehydrated thanks to a fever. The flu, he said, and then he chuckled and told Thorn he could expect to notice symptoms of his own within forty-eight hours.

He didn't care. All he knew was that the woman he wanted to build a life with was practically unconscious and it was his fault. He wanted her to wake up. He wanted to take her into his arms and love her doubts away. He knew she loved him, he just knew it. She had to. The certainty of his feelings for her engulfed him and yet he sensed it was only the beginning, that his love for her would grow through the years instead of diminish, that by the time he finally died he would be closer to her heart than to his own.

A light knock on the door startled him from his thoughts. He rose swiftly, sure the doctor had come back.

Natalie stood in the hall. She'd been crying. Thorn had seen his share of crying women, but no one did it like Natalie. While others appeared ravished and distraught, she grew more beautiful. This was when her eyes looked like well water, when her lower lip trembled, when perfect tears rested on high cheekbones as though glued permanently in place.

Without a word, she pushed past him and entered the room, stopping dead in her tracks when she spotted Alexandra's dark hair spilling over the pillow, the gold dress laid carefully over the back of a chair. She turned quickly to face Thorn. "It didn't take you long to find solace, did it?" she snapped.

"Keep your voice down. Better yet, get lost. The door is right over there."

Her manner changed instantly. She came toward him, her face downcast, contrite, her eyes flashing at him as she cast him quick, flirty looks. "Thorn, sweetie, I can't tell you how glad I am you found me."

He took a step away from her, disgusted with himself for ever having thought her appealing. "Go away," he said.

"You don't mean that," she said softly.

"Actually, I do. Get lost. Go find Conrad and ply your charms on someone who gives a damn."

Tears sprang to her eyes. "Conrad has left me. Oh, Thorn, you were right. He'll never leave his wife. Come on, sweetie, it's not too late, you know. I made a mistake, I admit it, but Thorn, you know what we had together." She ran her finger along his bare arm. "Thorn? I know it's not too late for us."

"I believe you called me a fool," he said dryly.

"Oh, sweetie, you know I just said that because of Conrad. He's so mean to me. You don't know what I've been through the last few days, how many times I wanted to call and ask you to come save me from him, to save me from myself."

The laugh came from deep in his belly. "I can only imagine the trials this man has put you through," he said, wiping tears from his eyes.

"That's right. Don't laugh at me, sweetie. You just don't understand what the last few days have been like. Conrad has forced me to stay. All I really wanted was to come back to you."

Thorn glanced at Alexandra. What a shame she was missing this performance! He repeated the last few lines to himself, attempting to commit them to memory so he could tell her about it when she was better. It was too much, just too much, and he erupted into laughter again.

"Don't be this way, sweetie. You still love me, I know you do—I can see it in your eyes."

"What you see in my eyes is utter confusion, Natalie. I just can't imagine why I was ever willing to settle for the likes of you. It truly astounds me."

* * *

Upon hearing laughter and voices, a woman's voice, Alex stirred. She opened weary eyes and gazed into the dark room. There was Thorn standing by the open door, and in front of him was Natalie, her hand outstretched, her voice pleading.

"I've always loved you, you know that," Natalie said. "Come on, baby, forgive me and let's go back to the way it was. You know how I feel about you."

Alex nodded internally. This, then, was how it would end. Thorn would see his Natalie reaching out to him and he wouldn't be able to resist. Alex was overcome with sadness. In a dream she'd just had, Thorn had talked about the stars and horses and flowers and she'd felt herself floating toward the most wonderful future. But he must have said those things to Natalie, not to her. It was so sad.

"Don't touch me," Thorn said, his voice harsh. "The only thing I know about you is that you're bad news. Now, before you awaken Alexandra, get the hell out of this room and don't ever darken my doorway again."

Natalie spat Alexandra's name. "What could you possibly see in that little nobody!"

"Everything," he said, as Alex felt a wave of warmth flow through her body. She watched as Thorn pulled Natalie to the door, pushed her into the hall and carefully closed the door on her.

Then he was at her side, kneeling by the pillow, running a cold cloth over her forehead. "I'm sorry, honey," he whispered.

She licked dry lips. "Is Natalie really gone?"

"For good," he said softly.

"You sent her away?"

"Don't sound so surprised. My taste in women has taken a marked turn for the better since I met you." He raised a glass of water to her lips. "Here, take a sip. The doctor said we had to get some fluids into you. You just have the flu, that's all. You're going to be okay in a couple of days.''

She took a drink of the cool water, then put her head back on the pillow. She stared up into his eyes, her mind a swirling mass of impressions, of feelings and images and words. It hurt to try to sort through them, it hurt to hunt for details. She said, ''It's just one thing after another with us, isn't it?''

He laughed softly. ''Isn't it great? Not the flu, but the adventure of it all. Listen, Alexandra, everything that has happened has kept us together. We've had nothing but good luck since the minute we took off together.''

She smiled, or at least she intended to smile. All she really knew was the touch of his hand on her forehead, and then his voice. ''I love you, Alexandra,'' he uttered against her skin. ''Marry me, darling.''

It was too soon to talk of marriage, she thought to herself as she stared into his eyes. Too soon, and yet...

''I love you, too,'' she mumbled.

''Am I your other half?'' he asked cautiously as though afraid of the answer.

She nodded.

''And you're mine,'' he said softly, his lips near hers.

''Don't kiss me,'' she mumbled. ''Germs—''

''To hell with germs,'' he murmured before his mouth claimed hers. Glory, glory, he loved her, or at least he thought he did. Time would tell....

Epilogue

Roger, the doorman at the Otter Point Inn, stood at attention under the awning in front of the hotel. It was December and it was cold outside. He was being promoted to a desk clerk position in February because Candy was resigning. Rumor had it Candy was chasing after old Alfie, the desk clerk who had worked here for years until a month ago when he'd moved to Florida. It was kind of hard to picture a dish like Candy wanting a dried-up old prune like Alfred, but then, you couldn't tell about people and love—even he knew that! At any rate, Roger just hoped he didn't die of pneumonia before he was moved inside to that cushy desk job.

As it was three days before Christmas, the inn was fairly busy with people who were arriving to spend their holiday in the plush confines of this four-star establishment. Still, there was something familiar about the Mercedes that rolled to a stop in front of him. Pink letters on the trunk said Just Married, and a long string of tin cans rattled on the pavement behind the car.

Roger opened the passenger door and the feeling of déjà vu increased. The woman he helped out of the car was wearing a straight, body-hugging wedding gown. Her dark hair was coiled on top of her head, making her look a little taller than she actually was. She was a real looker with deep blue eyes and delicate features that somehow struck a chord in his memory.

A man got out from behind the wheel and smiled at him.

"I remember you!" Roger said. "Last July, you were here on your honeymoon. Yeah, I remember the car."

The man exchanged a long look with the woman, and then they both broke out into laughter. As he placed a handsome black Stetson on his head, he said, "It was June, but who cares? We're here again on a...second...honeymoon." He joined the woman at the curb, his eyes devouring her as she stood there looking at him.

A second honeymoon just six months after the first, and with a wedding gown and everything? Odd. He kind of recalled Alfred telling everyone that their last honeymoon hadn't gone too well, that the man had been chasing after someone else. And didn't that lady down in the gift shop say something about this guy buying presents for another woman? Maybe that was it. Maybe they were trying to patch up their young marriage.

The guy was crazy! Why would anyone chase after another woman with a wife like that sitting in the room by herself?

Roger did a mental shrug. "Very good, sir. Hey, didn't I wash shaving cream off your car before? Want I should do it again? Hate to ruin that paint job—"

"Just leave it alone," the man said sternly, but with a glint of amusement in his eye. "I don't give a damn about the paint. Besides, I like the way it looks there, don't you, Alexandra?"

The bride's eyes got kind of misty looking; she bit her lip as she nodded.

The man handed him a twenty-dollar bill wrapped around a set of car keys; then he turned to the bride and effortlessly lifted her into his arms. "Ready, my darling?" he asked with a smile.

"Oh, Thorn." She laughed. She seemed to struggle to make her face look serious and added, "Ready for what?"

"Ready for me?" the man said, his voice suddenly husky. "Ready for *us?*"

She looked at him with such complete adoration that for the first time in Roger's life, he felt the stunning desire that someday a woman might look at him that way. The man lowered his face until their lips met and they melted into each other. The kiss went on and on, as though they were unaware that they weren't alone, as though they didn't care if anyone was watching them or not.

With an effort, Roger turned away, a smirk on his face. *Whoa! Hot stuff!* There may have been problems after the first wedding ceremony, but this time it promised to be a no-maid-service-please kind of interlude!

"The luggage is in the trunk," the man finally said. As Roger unlocked the trunk and took out the two matching leather bags, he watched the man carry the woman toward the etched doors, his back straight and strong, the woman's arms wrapped around his neck, her gown clinging to her legs. The man turned his back to the door and pushed it open himself. Roger knew he should hurry to help but he also sensed his help was neither needed nor would it be appreciated.

For one long second, Roger's gaze darted from the bride to the groom and back again. Their expressions were identical, focused on the other, soft and adoring and lit with anticipation.

"Have a great second honeymoon," he called to them with a chuckle.

The bride giggled against the man's shoulder. The man looked up at him and winked. "Don't worry about it," he said. "That's exactly what we plan to do."

* * * * *

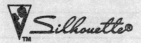

Take 4 bestselling love stories FREE
Plus get a FREE surprise gift!

Special Limited-time Offer

Mail to Silhouette Reader Service™

3010 Walden Avenue
P.O. Box 1867
Buffalo, N.Y. 14240-1867

YES! Please send me 4 free Silhouette Romance™ novels and my free surprise gift. Then send me 6 brand-new novels every month, which I will receive months before they appear in bookstores. Bill me at the low price of $2.67 each plus 25¢ delivery and applicable sales tax, if any.* That's the complete price and a savings of over 10% off the cover prices—quite a bargain! I understand that accepting the books and gift places me under no obligation ever to buy any books. I can always return a shipment and cancel at any time. Even if I never buy another book from Silhouette, the 4 free books and the surprise gift are mine to keep forever.

215 BPA A3UT

Name	(PLEASE PRINT)	
Address	Apt. No.	
City	State	Zip

This offer is limited to one order per household and not valid to present Silhouette Romance™ subscribers. *Terms and prices are subject to change without notice. Sales tax applicable in N.Y.

USROM-696 ©1990 Harlequin Enterprises Limited

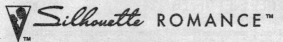

As seen on TV!
Free Gift Offer

With a Free Gift proof-of-purchase from any Silhouette® book,
you can receive a beautiful cubic zirconia pendant.

This gorgeous marquise-shaped stone is a genuine cubic
zirconia—accented by an 18" gold tone necklace.

(Approximate retail value $19.95)

Send for yours today...
compliments of *Silhouette®*

To receive your free gift, a cubic zirconia pendant, send us one original proof-of-purchase, photocopies not accepted, from the back of any Silhouette Romance™, Silhouette Desire®, Silhouette Special Edition®, Silhouette Intimate Moments® or Silhouette Yours Truly™ title available in February, March and April at your favorite retail outlet, together with the Free Gift Certificate, plus a check or money order for $1.65 U.S./$2.15 CAN. (do not send cash) to cover postage and handling, payable to Silhouette Free Gift Offer. We will send you the specified gift. Allow 6 to 8 weeks for delivery. Offer good until April 30, 1997 or while quantities last. Offer valid in the U.S. and Canada only.

Free Gift Certificate

Name: _____

Address: _____

City: _____ State/Province: _____ Zip/Postal Code: _____

Mail this certificate, one proof-of-purchase and a check or money order for postage and handling to: SILHOUETTE FREE GIFT OFFER 1997. In the U.S.: 3010 Walden Avenue, P.O. Box 9077, Buffalo NY 14269-9077. In Canada: P.O. Box 613, Fort Erie, Ontario L2Z 5X3.

FREE GIFT OFFER   084-KFD
ONE PROOF-OF-PURCHASE
To collect your fabulous FREE GIFT, a cubic zirconia pendant, you must include this original proof-of-purchase for each gift with the properly completed Free Gift Certificate.

084-KFD

In April 1997
Bestselling Author

DALLAS SCHULZE

takes her Family Circle series to new heights with

TESSA'S CHILD

In April 1997 Dallas Schulze brings readers a
brand-new, longer, out-of-series title featuring the
characters from her popular Family Circle miniseries.

When rancher Keefe Walker found Tessa Wyndham he
knew that she needed a man's protection—she was
pregnant, alone and on the run from a heartless past.
Keefe was also hiding from a dark past...but in one
overwhelming moment he and Tessa forged a family
bond that could never be broken.

Available in April wherever books are sold.

DSST

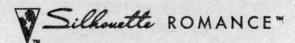

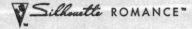

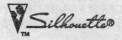

You're About to Become a

Privileged Woman

Reap the rewards of fabulous free gifts and benefits with proofs-of-purchase from Silhouette and Harlequin books

Pages & Privileges™

It's our way of thanking you for buying our books at your favorite retail stores.

Pages & Privileges ™

Harlequin and Silhouette—
the most privileged readers in the world!

For more information about Harlequin and Silhouette's PAGES & PRIVILEGES program call the Pages & Privileges Benefits Desk: 1-503-794-2499

Silhouette®

SR-PP23